THE

INLAND

SEA

Madeleine Watts

AN IMPRINT OF PUSHKIN PRESS

ONE, an imprint of
Pushkin Press
71–75 Shelton Street
London WC2H 9JQ

First published by ONE in 2020
This edition published 2021

1 3 5 7 9 8 6 4 2

ISBN 13: 978-1-91159-025-5

Designed and typeset by Tetragon, London
Printed and bound by CPI Group (UK) Ltd, Croydon CRO 4YY

www.pushkinpress.com

For Hayden,
and my mother.

Actually girls don't change, I think, from generation to generation. They're like moths blundering about in search of their fate. You know how moths hit you in the face—soft velvety things—and are sometimes killed... Nor do I think girls grow up into anything very different from what they were. They're still blundering about after they've promised to honour and obey. Oh, I don't mean they're dishonest—not all of them—but they're still quivering and preparing to discover something they haven't experienced yet.

—PATRICK WHITE,
THE VIVISECTOR

Australia has from the beginning of its short history meant something more to its new inhabitants than mere environment and mere land to be occupied, ploughed and brought into subjection. It has been the outer equivalent of an inner reality.

—JUDITH WRIGHT,
PREOCCUPATIONS IN AUSTRALIAN POETRY

Kassandra: "Who cares? The future is coming."

—AESCHYLUS,
AGAMEMNON (TRANS. ANNE CARSON)

I COULDN'T SLEEP AT NIGHT. The heat rose in the evenings, the old bricks of the house absorbed it, and after dark my bedroom felt as thick and quivering as an oven. Open windows didn't help. On the seven o'clock news there was always somebody making a show of frying an egg on the asphalt of an outer-suburbs driveway. Watch this! they would shout to the camera. Yolks slipped out onto the bitumen and sat trembling there beneath the burning Australian sun. The people on the news were always grinning, nearly naked but for a singlet or a pair of shorts, sweating into their sunglasses. Nobody ever ate the egg.

By the time the fireworks had blown up over the Harbour and the city was wasted and the New Year begun, I had handed in my final papers and my academic life was behind me. The open wilderness of adulthood stretched ahead like so much wasteland. During the sleepless days of that last hot summer I had no money and nothing to do, but the bus that left from Cleveland Street could get me to the beach in half an hour. The air along the coast in those months was full of seaweed and car exhaust and the fires that were burning on the edge of the city. Rounding the cliffs I could walk through the parklands and along the ocean path to the secluded rocks and boat racks of Gordon's Bay. I passed weeks there, stretched out on a towel, reading novels and jumping into the deep water when the heat became unbearable. In the end, they would say that this January was the hottest month on record, in the hottest year on record, although they've said that about every year since. But this was the last January I sweltered through before I left the city entirely. I don't know anything about those other summers.

The heatwave broke with a storm. The squall bore down from the Pacific, sweeping southerly winds across the city and snatching frangipani flowers from their branches. The convulsion of the storm struck in a way that seemed only natural, following as it did the tense weeks that seemed to justify the punch to the back of the head, the child left locked in the back seat of the car, the missing girl.

The morning after the storm arrived I lay on the rocks beside the bay, and at last I was able to sleep. When I woke up I was overheated, my body covered in sweat. I picked a way down the rocks and surveyed the brown storm-surge mucking up the edges of the water. I took a leap. The day was still, the rocks deserted, the splash could be heard all over the bay. I dived deep under the storm surge and closed my eyes and began to swim out. When I'd gone far enough into the depths, I turned and looked back to where I'd been. From above, the palms and bougainvillea erupted in great green and pink swarms from the cliff face like some madman's garden of Babylon. Seagulls circled overhead. I floated in the clear water in the middle of the bay and thought that I wouldn't be so afraid to be lost at sea. The smooth, blue expanse couldn't hurt me, not the one I imagined stretching out for miles and miles, all the way east to Valparaiso, north to California, the tips of Alaska and Russia and Japan, eternities away from here. The sun beat down. I tread water and spread out my arms. And I observed just then, as though waking not out of, but into, a nightmare, a long yellow and black thing swimming in the water.

The sun glinted on its scales, and it took me a moment to see it for what it actually was. I had never once seen one in the wild. When I was a child my mother had told me how deadly they could be. She had seen them, coiled on the seabed in the north of the country, and washed up on the beaches of the remote

Pacific islands she had visited with my father when they were happy together. That sea snakes rarely struck didn't make them any less threatening. If they bit you, the neurotoxic venom would begin to work through your limbs before you could make it to shore. Blurred vision, numb throat, a prickle in the soles of the feet, and then a burst of pain in every cell of your body, like a fire sweeping through the nervous system and destroying everything in its path. I looked at the water, flat and silent, all around me. I had swum out too far. The bay was empty. I knew that it was the most vulnerable parts of the body one needed to guard against. They bit you in the thin, fleshy spaces between your fingers and your toes. I drew my hands into fists. I kicked with my toes clenched. I swam towards the rocks, moving through the water as though I were punching it.

The snake had been carried into shore overnight, swept along from warmer depths by the storm.

The snake was weak, but weak things lash out.

Its body rose and fell with the lap of the tide, and it moved with its mouth open.

HEAT

I HAD MOVED TO REDFERN twelve months earlier, at the beginning of my Honours year at the university. When I first moved in my mother helped me drive my things across the city from Ashfield, where I'd grown up, and carry my boxes up the fifteen steps to the door. As she left that first day she looked around at the old terraces and the old Greek lady next door watching her husband watering the tomato plants, and the group of men loitering on the corner by the housing commission apartment blocks. She squeezed my arm and walked down the staircase to her car. Be careful, she said. Please. We had never lived apart before, and she believed the place was dangerous. She was concerned about the mould that grew beneath the skirting boards and she was sceptical about the efficacy of the cast-iron security door and she was afraid, more than anything, of the neighbourhood and its people.

Redfern still had the reputation of being a sordid area of Sydney, even if it was not as dangerous as it had once seemed. The suburb was filled with decaying Victorian terraces and housing commission towers where graffiti caked the open door-ways. Overdoses still trembled in the car park behind Surry Hills Shopping Village when I passed by with Coles bags full of carrots and hummus and rice. Bed sheets covered windows. Iron lace rusted into the pavement. Verandas were converted into kitchens without the council much caring. But things were changing. The junkies weren't gone, and neither were the indigenous commu-nities in The Block. Students and artists in search of cheap rent lived there, as ever they had. But by the time I moved in there were cocktail bars and cafés and seven-dollar loaves of bread. On the edges of the neighbourhood floorboards were being

polished and courtyards were being landscaped. Old factories had been demolished. High-rises were rising. A television newsreader living on the eastern fringe suggested that his side of the neighbourhood be renamed South Dowling to spare it from the stigma associated with the rest of Redfern.

The house where I lived was on Elizabeth Street, far from the South Dowling side. All the terraces on my side of the street were built so that they were elevated above the foot traffic, as though the original architects had been afraid of the squalor they suspected of festering at street level. As though the cockroaches couldn't fly through windows open that high. Each house was reached by a staircase of fifteen steps, spread at intervals along a sloping incline patched with vegetation and cement. The cockroaches still got in.

The Elizabeth Street house was old. There were forever cobwebs in the corners of the living room and an orange mould that bloomed in the bathtub. The green paint on the skirting boards had begun to peel away to reveal something black. The washing machine had a sticker at the base that read "Made in West Germany", and of the three of us who lived in the house none of us had been alive before the Berlin Wall fell. I lived upstairs in the front room and I was higher than every tree and building built around me.

The men I lived with had gone to high school with my friend Maeve, and I never knew them particularly well, not in all the time I lived there. So it was in the bedroom that I spent most of my time. I tacked postcards of Carol Jerrems and Bill Henson photographs to the walls and hung a pink paper lantern over the bare light bulb. My bed was covered by a yellow eiderdown and jutted out into the centre of the room. When I moved in, I supposed I'd be staying.

*

There was a square hole cut into the wall behind my bed, which had once been a fireplace. Somebody, long before I got there, had taped up the flue with a piece of cardboard. When the weather turned windy, black dust would sometimes breach the barrier and turn up in the hollow white space behind my pillows. The pillows too, would fall into the fireplace-hollow during rough sleep, or rough sex. The fireplace bothered me. Sometimes I could hear the sound of something that wasn't the wind or shifting cardboard, something that might have been an animal, but anyway sounded alive.

On my first night in the house I tried to remove the piece of cardboard in the chimney. Somebody had stuck it to the plaster with pieces of masking tape. When I prodded at it the cardboard flipped out and along with it a mound of dirt and soot. Once the soot had settled I peered into the flue. Its edges were lined with newspapers, yellow at the edges before they blackened and became indistinguishable. I reached out and picked away at them. I could make out one of the pages, just barely. A marriage announcement for a man and a woman, the wedding held at St Barnabas' Church on Broadway, in the winter of 1932. A jolt of air sent forth another tumble of dirt and the marriage announcement disintegrated in my fingers. I reached for the cardboard. I taped the chimney back up, and left the newspaper in fragments on the floor.

Now, a year later, the money I had saved was rapidly disappearing. I wrote sometimes, for magazines and literary journals and the street press, but it was never enough to keep me in rent. My student allowance had dried up with the end of semester and the official termination of my student status. I was paying full fare on the train.

In a word, I was drifting.

I had spent four years of university preparing to spend the rest of my life in the sandstone sanctum of academia. For years before I enrolled I had passed by the golden buildings on the hill in Camperdown and imagined it to be a kind of utopia where men and women spent days on end walking the flagstones and making sense of all that was senseless. I thought it was where I belonged, and I had no plans that extended much beyond the reaches of its architecture. All year, my thesis supervisor had spent our weekly meetings laying the groundwork for my doctorate proposal. She said more women were needed to stop the discipline turning stale. Young women with good minds. Like me. But by the time November arrived I had applied for nothing, had written no proposals, had already missed deadlines. I sat in her office on that final afternoon surrounded by stacks of ungraded essays she had organized into neat rows across the rose-print carpet. A poster of Nick Cave glowered down from the corkboard above her desk. I looked out through her window to the already fruiting trees in the courtyard of the Woolley building, and everything looked brighter, and more vivid, as though it might contain significance. Because I had never thought that I might miss it before. My supervisor hummed, and conceded, when I pointed out how neurotically inarticulate and exhausted I had become, that it might be best to wait a year.

I walked out of my supervisor's office and down the long hallway to the wide-open exit. I sat down on the brick wall and lit a cigarette, although it was not a designated smoking area, and considered how senseless the last year I had spent in the Woolley building seemed suddenly to be. The university was very tranquil at this time of day, and there was nobody to see me. My legs were crossed too tightly, and I imagine if someone had passed by and noticed I would have looked as though I were disappearing into

the bushes growing up against the wall. I did not appear, from the outside, to have entered any sort of wilderness. But half a year ago I had sat on this same brick wall outside the Woolley building waiting for a man, with a sense of anticipation and purpose that, by this afternoon, I had lost entirely. Its essential train of logic had been exposed as absurd, along with all the patterns of reason that I had believed I could rely on. I did not know what the future would look like anymore. I smoked the cigarette and the sun beat down and then I walked to Glebe, to buy the first novel I would read on those rocks in the summer at Gordon's Bay.

By January the money was gone and I needed a job. The heat was relentless. We were told that the intense weather signalled the end of "stationarity". The thousand-year storms no longer happened every thousand years. They seemed to occur yearly now, maybe more, along with the heat, the fire and the floods. I went to bed at night with all the windows open. Bats conspired outside in the trees.

Directly across the street from my bedroom there was a car mechanic's called Sydney Prestige. They announced their "excellence in European auto service" across the awning, but they were a constant source of angry arguments from irate BMW drivers claiming negligence and fraud. A paperbark tree grew out the front. Its roots broke open the pavement and tripped over the kids and the drunks who passed by. When the summer began, I tried to take charge of the windows. I dismantled the plastic blinds, bought curtain rods, and hung long strips of white fabric over the glass. I had thought that the white light they collected in the afternoon sun would quieten the room. But all through December the white fabric got soaked by afternoon storms and turned brown in the exhaust from the buses that stopped on the

street below. After a while the curtains were filthy, and I stopped closing them when I undressed in the mornings. The men working across the street at the mechanic's would look at me when I passed naked in front of the open windows, but nobody ever called out or said anything.

When I was a child a high fence had shielded my bedroom window, but my mother would insist that I close the blinds when I took my clothes off. People might see, she would say, looking into the thick shrubs that lined the fence. The seeing—it was evident to my mother—was a danger. But I never felt endangered when I undressed in front of the open windows in Redfern, and in the year before I left Sydney it stopped occurring to me that perhaps I ought to.

I T WAS MAEVE who told me that there were openings at the call centre. I thought perhaps the job would be stressful, but I reasoned that it would only ever be temporary. And besides, the fact that Maeve already worked there all but guaranteed that they would hire me.

I was interviewed in a beige room on the seventh floor of a building in Darling Harbour, in the office of the country's largest labour hire company. Four women were hired that day, and I was the only one who had finished high school. I figured out later that the hiring policy was based on the likelihood that the applicants would stick around, and the four of us didn't look like we were doing anything else. As we left the group-interview stage and emerged from the elevator into the rush-hour foot traffic on Market Street, a girl with bleached hair and three inches of black roots told me she had failed the spelling test, but was pleased that they'd told her she'd receive a call in a couple of days. She made a sound that I think was meant to be laughter. I told her I had studied Literature, and she asked me if that meant books.

The actual office was located on the other side of the city. It spanned the first floor of a skyscraper on the corner of Bathurst and Elizabeth Streets, overlooking Hyde Park. Technically, the office was on the same street that I lived on, and I could walk to work, but my stretch of Elizabeth Street was all kebab shops and bars and brothels, as though in the half hour it took to walk down Elizabeth Street to my house the city was gradually loosening its belt and taking off its clothes.

The proximity of the office to Hyde Park made it easy for me to imagine that I might enjoy the job, and in the morning

it was soothing to see busy, professional people making their way through crowds that streamed steadily along beneath the Moreton Bay figs that lined the street. But the managers drew the blinds at dusk and, besides, most of the time you were not sitting near the window, and the window was not much of a reprieve from the trilateral smog-coloured workstations and the fluorescent lighting and the constant ringing of phones.

After a morning of training that encompassed company policy and instructions on how to navigate the procedures and regulations of the nation's largest telecommunications company, a woman with corkscrew curls and broken teeth named Pat showed me how to use the desktop computers where we received the calls. I was handed a headset and placed at a workstation. I started answering the phone.

People were meant to dial ooo but every single person who called was in a panic, and some people who had been confused by watching too much American television would slip up and dial 911 instead. It didn't matter. The calls came through anyway. Every emergency phone call in the country came through to centres in either Sydney or Melbourne. In these centres spoke the first voices a person would hear in a crisis. After establishing whether someone was in need of the police, the ambulance or the fire brigade, it was my job to determine a person's state and town and connect the calls through to the dispatch centres.

The first one wasn't too bad. Emergency police, fire or ambulance? I asked.

The man on the other end of the line said, Ah, ah, police. There's been a crash on the M4.

What state and town is the emergency in?

Ah shit. Well, it's the M4. Um, there's a sign for Wet 'N' Wild up ahead, so what's that? Merrylands?

Merrylands in which state?

Oh, New South Wales.

Connecting to the police for Merrylands, New South Wales.

The line rang twice, the police answered, I read them the job number, waited for the police and the man to begin talking, pressed the arrow key three times to the right, hit enter, and hung up. It was even boring.

The calls went on like that, until late afternoon. At a quarter to five a red siren above the windows that overlooked the park began to blare. It means there's high traffic, Pat explained, with all her curls and her teeth.

A car crash, a breakdown, asphyxia, a wrong number, a misdial, a car crash and then screaming.

Ambulance. I need the ambulance the ambulance the ambulance.

What state and town is the emergency in?

Werribee. Victoria. I need an ambulance an ambulance.

And the phone rang, and it rang, and the woman screamed once more, and I connected to another number, and told her the ambulance service would answer as soon as they could, and it rang twelve times while she screamed and the siren blared above the windows while the rush-hour crowds streamed through Hyde Park. But eventually the ambulance answered. And eventually the siren went quiet.

In my first afternoon working at Triple Zero, I took calls from angry drivers, an old man with chest pains, a white woman who didn't like the look of the brown boys on the corner, teenagers fucking around after school, a woman hiding from her ex-boyfriend under the bed, and a mother whose baby had turned blue.

The phone calls came from everywhere in the country, at every time of day. In a few months, I learnt to spell the names of

all the tricky towns, regardless of the fact that my knowledge of their location on the map was usually hazy. Towns with hidden "u"s got to be my favourite—Aurukun. Wauchope. Nhulunbuy. Gradually, I learnt the dangerous parts of every city by the number of calls coming through. I winced hearing the names of places I had never been. Mount Isa and Eagleby, Bourke and Mount Druitt, Narre Warren and Frankston, Tennant Creek and Alice Springs. I made a vow that I would never set foot in Cairns or Townsville. If callers didn't give us a location, or the noise on the phone sounded like screaming or struggle, we could connect to the capital city of whatever state we thought the call was coming from. There was data on the screen, but it didn't reveal much. We could see neither names nor precise locations that might illuminate a caller's emergency, only their state and phone number. Calls for domestics on Thursday Island, a location so remote it was practically Papua New Guinea, could be referred to the Brisbane police dispatch centre, regardless of the place being half a continent away. Because it was, after all, in Queensland.

A shift of eight hours involved being dropped into emergencies and pulled out, hearing only pieces of whatever the story was, up to fifty times an hour. We asked the questions we were meant to ask, we did it quickly, we stuck to the script. The script we were taught on our first day was meant to shield us from distress. If all went as planned, the person calling didn't tell us about the fire raging down their cliff or the body they'd discovered at the bottom of a gully. We waited to hear the caller engage with the paramedic or the firefighter and then quietly hung up before hearing the details. We were not meant to hear the problem. We were not meant to hear the woman howl for the baby turning blue in her arms. But the woman howling couldn't know that I was not the person she was meant to tell. She didn't know that I couldn't help her.

The centres never closed. We worked in eight-hour shifts around the clock, and so we tended to fall into three categories: the morning group, peopled mostly by senior citizens in orthopaedic shoes; the overnight shift, filled mostly with erratic cosplayers, the autistic, obese or formerly incarcerated; and the afternoon shift, where the rest of us ended up. There were actors and sculptors, high-school dropouts, TAFE students, the listless, the aimless and those who had fallen into the job because it seemed like a worthwhile way station between one thing and the next. Pat, who trained me, had been an environmental lawyer, and I never learnt why she was a lawyer no longer.

The shifts we worked could change according to the whims of the contractor we were technically employed by. Some weeks would be filled with shifts that began at four in the afternoon and ended at midnight, followed by a shift that began at five in the morning and ended at one.

Without the windows, there was very little to look at or do in the call centre. Televisions were mounted on the walls on either side of the room. They were never turned off, but they didn't have sound. We were not allowed to watch subtitled programmes. We were not allowed to read, to have our phones or to eat. We were not trusted with distractions. To fill the time we talked to those at the phones around us, but nobody talked about the calls. Why should you care? Pat asked, whenever, in the first week, I expressed distress.

Occasionally I would lean over to Maeve if we were working at the same time, and try to tell her about something strange or funny or horrific.

I don't want to hear it, she said each time. She had worked there for four years.

When I'd first met Maeve in our Honours seminar a year

earlier, she had shown me the tattoo of a heart she had got in Oaxaca from a man with a dirty needle. She had been twenty when she'd had her wrist tattooed, and she was only three years older now, but she had begun to hide the heart with bracelets and long sleeves. Maeve had short hair and a nose ring, and when I'd met her she had stood outside the Woolley building with one hip pushed against the low brick wall and told me that she was probably a lesbian. But she gradually eased away from the assuredness of that first heady identification, so that by the time we have reached now, she had recently described herself to me as seven eighths straight. The tattoo in Oaxaca would be the last of the risks she ever really took. Maeve was dating a Jewish boy who lived by Centennial Park with his parents. His friends were music producers and private-school junkies and convicted felons. Maeve lingered in their world like she belonged there, but she didn't do drugs, and she believed in the rules, and she was planning on applying to law school. She had a plan for the future, and she knew precisely what it looked like. I tried to talk to her about the emergencies. But she was not interested in my feelings, or my thoughts. I never saw her shake after hanging up the phone.

During my first week, Pat with the terrible teeth and corkscrew curls tried to explain the way the place worked. Some people can't hack it, she said. They take the calls personally, and those are the ones that are out of here in three weeks. You've got to get it into your head that this is just a job.

I nodded. I did not want to be one of the weak ones who couldn't hack it. She explained the centre's social dynamics. She pointed out the couple in the far corner who were having an affair. She pointed to the middle-aged man who went to Thailand every year to get a hair transplant. She pointed out the pair of

skinny men with soft bellies. The dumbest fucks here, she said. They knew nothing about anything. Climate change is real, she advised me as I finished another call. I nodded. She told me about the bleaching of the Great Barrier Reef, the melting of the permafrost, the rising incidences of freak weather activities, as though I believed it wasn't happening. The glaciers were melting, she said. And I nodded. The sea would rise by a hundred metres, maybe more. The Maldives were already sinking below the surface. The oceans were acidifying. The state government was soon to begin fracking the Great Artesian Basin, the underground water source that covered a quarter of the continent, the real-deal shadow of the mythical inland sea the nineteenth century had earnestly supposed was Out There. The water would be poisoned. The land would dry up. The ground would quake. There was no turning back. And those dumb fucks, she pointed again, all they give a shit about is footy and lunch.

I nodded.

Hey, you've got to answer in three seconds, you know, she gestured to the screen, where the incoming call icon was displayed. If you don't answer within three seconds, you're gone.

It occurred to me only later that perhaps I was not suited to this type of work, not having much in the way of appropriate boundaries between myself and the rest of the world.

On the first free day after my initial week at Triple Zero, I woke up near noon and found that there were no coffee beans left in the biscuit tin by the stove. I pulled on a too-big jumper over a tatty dress and left the house without showering. Outside, I fumbled with the keys to the iron security door. A week earlier I had tried to leave the house to find that, overnight, somebody had wrenched the heavy couch underneath the front window across our door to bar our exit. There was no way to push it out of the

way. I woke up my housemate Paul. With Joe, who lived in the room next to mine but who I barely ever saw, I watched Paul climb out my window and scale the drainpipe. We watched him jump from the awning and push the couch back into place and use his key to open up the door and walk back into the house.

The couch barring the door seemed like an augury. It seemed to confirm my suspicion that everything contained the potential for menace. After a week taking emergency calls, everything did. The Greek lady next door was sitting beneath the trellised grape vine that grew over our stairwell to the street, but she turned away from me as I locked the iron security door and pretended to organize the wool in her sewing basket. For a moment I saw myself from her perspective—the knotted hair and rumpled clothes—and I realized that I looked quite as "wild" to her eyes as the kind of people the architects had been afraid of when they'd built these houses up above the street. And this troubled me, because I wanted the lady and her husband next door to like me. I walked by her and turned left under the dappled light of the trees, towards Redfern Street and the cafés with their croissants and good coffee. As I walked I couldn't help but take everything personally. Every billboard. Every flyer in the gutter. A woman on the street by the florist saw me and called her husband to hurry into their idling car, slamming the door shut. The car seemed to veer towards me. Every driver I saw had unreliable wrists. The man who owned the Italian deli watered the laneway pot plants with his back to me. On the corner of Redfern Street an ibis perched atop a rubbish bin opened the big black garden shears of its beak as I passed. There were magpies, which I also took personally. In the corner of my vision I sensed them preparing to swoop at my head.

After just a week I had already began to adjust to a life where there was no time to analyse information if you were going to

be one of the ones who could hack it, and where three seconds was all it took to get gone. I was primed for gut reactions. I was attuned to all the reflex tests of the psyche: hot-takes and pop-ups and "Act Now" demands.

In January of the year I left Sydney I became afraid of walking too close to the gutter and the cars that veered around corners too quickly. I was afraid of cyclists, people in tracksuits by traffic lights, afraid of staircases and lit cigarettes and power lines. I was afraid of men. I was afraid of just about everything.

I RAN INTO LACHLAN near Redfern Station. I had not seen or heard from him in months. And then, on a Wednesday night, I passed him as he was pushing through the turnstiles and into the street. I pretended not to notice he was there. But in the reflection of the shop windows I watched him follow me down the street as I walked towards an ATM.

He caught up with me.

He leant on the ATM as I withdrew two twenty-dollar bills and asked me why I hadn't said hello.

I had supposed he would not want to speak to me again, and I had not wanted to see his face, or the expression I supposed I would see there—surprise, then amusement, then dread. Because he was afraid of me, for reasons I never entirely understood. But I did not say that then.

Instead, I asked him how he had been, and he told me about the desk the university had given him on the bottom floor of Fisher Library upon acceptance into his doctoral programme. At night, he said, they turned off the overhead lamps to save energy. After that, the only lights that remained were the orbs over the occupied desks. Four or five people sitting beneath lonely jaundiced spotlight. And then, he said, if you haven't moved for a while because you have been, say, sitting holding your head in your hands, that light switches off as well.

He was writing his doctorate on Patrick White, which made sense. Lachlan must have been the only man in Sydney to sleep beneath a framed portrait of the nation's greatest unread novelist. He might have been the only man in the world who had ever done such a thing.

We fell into step with one another. The air hummed with

mosquitoes and crickets. Bats took flight through the bright orange dusk. We followed along Redfern Street past doors of pubs where the noise tumbled out into the streets, by chicken shops and galleries, across the smashed glass of shuttered storefronts, past terraces with only the screen door shut. It seemed like some of those houses were remnants of an older city. Bougainvillea choked the windows, tree roots unsettled the pavement, and the streets in the last light of evening looked like the return of the bush was being kept only barely in reserve. Water dripped from the gutters and drains. It seemed as though the whole city was wet.

We did not say the kinds of things you might normally say to somebody you had not seen in months. His name was Lachlan, except it wasn't, not really. I have given new names to everybody I once knew, everybody expect myself.

What's this dress? he asked. I haven't seen this dress before.

Why would you? I said, and followed him into a bar.

It's nice. This, what, this lace thing? He brushed a finger across the fabric, beneath which lay my collarbone. Sweat rolled down my chest and soaked into the polyester lining beneath the lace, but the dress was black and he could not see what a mess I was underneath my clothes.

He ordered whisky and found a table at the back in the path of the overhead ceiling fan. We began to drink together in the dark.

You almost didn't talk to me earlier, did you? I asked.

He thumbed the rim of the soap-stained glass.

I really thought about it.

I'm glad you did.

So am I.

I'm sorry for the way things were last year.

He shook his head. We are the victims of the stories we tell ourselves, he said. Even when they might be true.

*

I had met Lachlan for the first time at the beginning of the year before. We were in an Honours seminar together, studying neglected Australian books written by highly strung misanthropes. There were two men in the class and five women.

I was not sure of his name for the first month of the semester, so he came to seem only half-real. Always a stranger, he was a kind of blank canvas I could paint on at will. Eventually, of course, I did learn his name. By then I had determined that I had never met any man as vivid or as compelling as him. Lachlan had read everything, and although he was only twenty-three he already spoke with the weary authority of an old man. He had won every award, had published poetry and essays, had his plays performed by middle-range theatre companies. He spoke about the prose of Patrick White in a way that made me want to read every one of his novels, and I did.

Because there were so few of us studying in the Australian literature stream of the English department, we were together, in all of our classes, all of the time, and quickly close although none of us had known one another before that year. I met Maeve at the beginning of that semester, fresh with her tattoo, Cate the neatly dressed poet, and one or two others whose names are lost to me now, figures who have faded into the slipstream like so many minor characters. Every Friday morning we would all file into the dark, vaulted seminar room at the top of the Woolley building, and every Friday Lachlan was late. Twenty minutes in, there would be a pounding of footsteps coming up the stairs, and he would slip in, flushed, holding a cup of coffee, and take a chair closest to the door. He looked as though he had recently returned from having spent time in the desert. Forearms still brown from the sun, he had blue eyes and sandy-coloured hair and a peculiar grace to the slope and curve of his torso when he sat.

*

32

One afternoon one of the five women, a dull, linnet-coloured girl whose name now escapes me, complained about having to read *The Night, The Prowler* for the following week. At the end of the class, slipping our things back into bags, I defended White, who I allowed was dense and serious and unfashionable. But his books are beautiful, I told her.

Yes, Lachlan said, very quietly, from behind my shoulder. He was looking at me with all that quiet and focus, although I did not know then whether he agreed with me or not.

I was always very attracted to you, he would tell me later. From the start.

The smell of cigarettes followed him out of the room, as well as something else. A warm, deep thing I couldn't quite place. A promise. Through the open windows I could see the leaves were turning. As we reached the staircase Lachlan turned to me and asked if I would like to get something to eat.

We bought coffee at Ralph's by the university gym and walked outside to sit on the steps of the Old Teachers' College. We had an hour, and I did not know quite how I would fill it. I thought that his body gave a nice shape to the staircase, but that was not anything I could have said. I had been rendered temporarily wordless. He told me about the play he was rehearsing, using his cigarette to emphasize the point he was making. It was about fathers, and bloodlines, and the burden of inheritance. His own father had died when he was twelve, and that fact made Lachlan more romantic and sympathetic about fathers than my own life has ever allowed me to be. Weeks later, he would let me read the play. It was good. I think now that if he had been a bad storyteller, I could never have gone on with him, or at least not for as long as I did.

*

He told me once about his childhood. From the age of five to twelve Lachlan went to a school where there was chapel twice weekly and prayer before class. Stained-glass windows lined each side of the chapel, and each one depicted a saint. Beyond the school fence, and through the coloured glass that obscured the surroundings, grew a grove of paperbark trees. It had seemed self-evident to him, for the longest time, that this was where paper came from. That adults simply stripped the paper off the tree and walked away with it. He could never try it out because the trees were on the out-of-bounds side of the fence, and by the time he got a scholarship to the more elite school an hour's train ride away he had already forsaken the belief that what he needed might grow on trees, and he had lost his belief in the sanctifying power of the stained-glass windows and their saints.

I remembered the paperbark tree that had been on the edge of the playground in my primary school, half a city away from his. I would sometimes spend the length of the recess break alone, stripping the tree of its bark and shuffling the pieces together in neat piles, wondering why I could never get them as thin and rectangular as the sheets they handed out in the classroom. I assumed that it was my deficiency. I wasn't doing it right. I hadn't learnt to tear the bark off in the correct way.

That's cute, he said when I told him.

We had both believed in paper coming from paperbark trees, and at the time this felt important, and perhaps I mention it now because it still does. It is not often that such sad, strange children find one another as adults.

In the first week of Honours classes, I had walked home with Maeve, and she had mocked Lachlan. The way he smoked, the way he spoke, the things he spoke about. She thought he was affected. Because Lachlan was from a place in Sydney where

the men became construction workers and the women became hairdressers, but he sounded for all the world like he'd been plucked straight out of Oxbridge. How he learnt to speak that way in Engadine was a mystery never solved.

Maeve was right about his speech. But where she saw affectation I found comfort. He had a deep, smooth timbre to his voice. Like a mid-century newscaster, some formative father. It was Home. When he spoke to me, I found that his voice could unify every disparate formless thing, everything that caused me anxiety, everything I didn't understand. As he spoke the rivers swelled, the water tanks refilled, the pollutants and the sea snakes were cleansed from the storm surge, the Maldives rose above the waterline, the melting glaciers were restored to their rightful form. It seemed, as he spoke, that with him I was safe.

Getting windy, he said that first afternoon on the steps of the Old Teachers' College.

Yes, I said, it feels like it, looking at the trees, as though I had just noticed that the leaves were moving.

Yeah. It's strange weather.

I nodded. And then we stood up and walked back to the Woolley building to our next seminar. We sat separately, at either ends of the room.

We found ways to be around one another. *I'm here, come by if you're close.* I told him about the songs I liked. He bought bottles of wine for the two of us to share. He texted me photographs of interesting passages from the copies of books he kept by his bed.

"Perhaps because a rare commodity, water played a leading part in my developing sexuality. I was always throwing off clothes to bathe, either at the artesian bore during a pause from mustering, the water ejaculating warm and sulphurous out of the earth, or in

the river flowing between the trunks of flesh-coloured gums, to a screeching flick-knife commentary of yellow-crested cockatoos."

It's from *Flaws in the Glass*, Lachlan wrote below the photograph. Because you said you like swimming.

The first time I kissed him we were in the side passage of his house in Erskineville. He pushed me away. The next day he said it was because I had been too drunk. And in truth, I never remembered first kissing him.

This was a time in my life when it was difficult to stop drinking once I'd started. I understood that the drinking made me vulnerable, perhaps even pathetic, but I didn't stop. I didn't stop because part of me believed that if I went on and on, past the point where my legs lost their coordination, when the syllables of words crumbled in my mouth, and my thoughts escaped the prison of coherence, then I would come out on the other side of the black-out into a new world. Maybe not better than the one I'd left, but new, and just for me.

When we finally went to bed together I undressed, turned the light out by his door, got under the bedclothes and lay beside him.

Do you always come to bed with your tights on? he asked.

I shook my head. I did not usually sleep with my tights on. I just didn't want to seem brazen.

He coaxed the tights down my hips and examined my face. His fingers traced out the curves and ridges, as though there were a difficult cartography to my features that he was trying to learn by hand.

I had never been looked at with such focus. It was the same focus he had on his face when he read, and what person doesn't want to be read? And I was still open like a wound, back then,

still formless, or forming, but young enough to believe in all the romance of the poetry I loved, the kind of belief that puts you on a river and makes you follow it down.

One night cutting through the Eveleigh railway yards towards his house he stopped me and made me turn to look at him. A violet light from the city skyline cast a glow through the shapes of the retired train carriages. I tripped over broken cement and dead-end tracks.

He held my face in his hands. Hey, he said. I think you're somebody who hasn't been loved nearly as much as they ought to have been.

Don't, I said. That's not. Don't. But I did not mean for him to stop kissing me, and he knew, because he did not stop.

Are you OK? he asked.

Yes, I said, and he looked very serious. Why?

Are you pregnant?

It was a strange place for such a conversation. The Eveleigh railway yards was a part of the city you could easily imagine yourself being taken, held down, raped, murdered, a scream-absorbing place where nobody would find a trace of you until the unbearable break of day.

He ended it as we walked up Cleveland Street to City Road on a Friday afternoon. It had been two days since the procedure. The disorientation of the anaesthetic had faded away, and most of the pain, but the bleeding had started in the shower that morning. Viscous dark red clots that slid down the inside of my thighs and dispersed in the pooling water.

I waited. We were almost at the intersection.

Then he opened his mouth. He began to speak. And it didn't matter what he was saying so much as the sound of his voice,

and the way it struck something warm and deep that dismantled me. His hand broad on my back. The things he had said in the Eveleigh railway yards.

I'm going to start seeing somebody, Lachlan said. Somebody else.

Oh. Right, I breathed. We had only been doing whatever it was that we were doing for two months, maybe less when I counted it all up. We'd never talked about what it was. We continued to walk up the hill. His hands were pushed deep into his pockets.

Just don't let it be somebody I know, I said.

He was quiet for a moment. He smoked a cigarette and he did not touch me.

I just think this woman is really worth trying for. You know, I usually fuck things up. But I'm going to try. I want to be a good man, with her. *Good*. And who knows, I might fuck it up again. But I really need to try with her.

OK, I said.

I think now that I had waited for years to be disassembled like I was in that moment. I thought being hurt would give my life an interesting kind of texture, the way good surfers are always marked by the scrapes and scars of battles fought with the waves. I believed it would give me something to write about.

Now, five months later, in the back of a bar in Redfern I opened my mouth to speak but he shook his head, looking up towards the opening door and the first glimpses of a pleated dress and a completely dry and guileless pretty face. Cate, the neatly dressed poet from our Australian literature Honours seminar he had wanted, in the end, more than me.

Or no. He would object. I misquote him.

This is what he actually said: I want both of you in completely different ways.

Although it seems now that the things he said mattered less than the way I received them. There is so much that I cannot fully remember, but I can hear him speak even now. For the rest of my life I will be able to recall his voice, the sheer density and tenor of the sound and all the ways in which it affected me. As a child it always seemed to me that part of the pleasure of reading a book was the freedom the reader had to imagine a person or a place in any way they chose. But I am selfish. I do not want you to imagine freely. I want you to be able to hear his voice as I did then—his voice, and nobody else's. Except my talent for description fails me now. Because all I can convey is an indefinite shape of a man saying Hey you, as I stood up to go, and making it sound like there was only one "you" in the world, and he did not want to see her leave.

O NE AFTERNOON before a six p.m. to two a.m. shift, as I walked up Elizabeth Street towards work, my phone vibrated against my elbow in my bag.

Maybe this is a dumb thing to say, but I'm glad we're speaking lately. I was worried maybe we weren't, generally.

I let the text linger on the lock screen while I considered its meaning. Yes, me too, I eventually replied.

In the call centre, the silent television broadcast a special half-hour news segment devoted to the heatwave gripping the city. The news crews were assembled at Bondi Beach. Cameras panned across glistening bodies, the waves, a woman fanning herself with a magazine. Bloody hot, mouthed a surfer when asked for his thoughts. Ambulance crews raced towards Circular Quay and Parramatta to tend to the elderly, the pregnant and the very young. In the western suburbs dogs and babies were discovered comatose after five minutes left inside locked cars. A Bubble O'Bill melted into the hand that held it. Children raised under drought conditions ran squealing through sidewalk sprinklers, the use of which was forbidden by state law. At Taronga Zoo, the lions were given milk-flavoured ice blocks. Carrot-flavoured ice was fed to the zebras. In Penrith, for the first time in living memory, the cricket was cancelled due to the heat.

On the phones there were calls for firefighters. Fires had spread across the south coast, from Bega to Cooma, to Tarcutta and Dean's Gap. More than 135 were burning across the state, forty of which were uncontained. A woman calling from Lane Cove told me she wanted to confirm with the fire service that she had chosen to go instead of stay. I lived through the fires of

'94, she told me. It's like a war zone. Smoke everywhere. I'm not going through that again.

Every part of me wanted to tell her that I too could remember the fires of '94. Remembered the smoke and the heat and the roads blocked off and no way home. But I was not allowed. I connected her to the fire brigade for Lane Cove, New South Wales.

Instead, in the notebook I kept beside me, I wrote down "Fires, '94, like a war zone".

In those first weeks at Triple Zero I had realized that if you sat at a station out of view of the managers, you could hide a phone in the headset box we all kept in our lockers when we were not at work. Everyone did. Most people used their phones to text or play games. Mostly, I used my phone to read. The reading, I thought, would keep me tethered to writing, to academia, to the life of the mind I thought was more important than being in the call centre. I read political analysis and book reviews and long articles about climate disaster. I equipped myself with facts and stories, which I thought functioned just as well as conversation might. I wrote the facts down in a notebook, for safekeeping. The notebook was not against the rules, and so could be out in the open beside the computer monitor, whereas the phone had to be hidden at all times.

I read and wrote down, in those weeks, that a wasting plague was afflicting the starfish of the Western Pacific coast. The illness started in the waters off Washington State, but had spread from Alaska, all the way down to San Diego. The starfish first developed a white discolouration, and then began to grow soft, until they turned to goo. The starfish were disintegrating for no reason anybody could seem to explain.

I wrote too that the Roman god Vulcan was the god of fire and volcanoes. It was understood that volcanic eruptions were a

sign of Vulcan's anger each time he learnt that Venus, his wife, had been found fucking someone else.

I wrote down this passage from an essay by David Wojnarowicz: "I am fearful or something more than fear: it's something in the landscape surrounding the cities and smaller towns between here and the coast, something *out there* that feels so empty and it is not made of earth or muscle or fur; it's like a pocket of death but with no form other than the light one might cast upon its trail of fragments."

I thought this was interesting.

Facts and passages like these seemed pertinent to my general condition. I had tried to bring up the facts in conversation, but Maeve had taken me to task. I explained that I was just trying to join in. I didn't want to seem quiet or unfriendly.

People like to talk about television and lunch and their relationships, she told me. If you're stuck, talk about the weather.

But I do talk about the weather, I responded.

Not your *kind* of weather, said Maeve. Normal weather.

Now I had taken to using the notebook every time I came upon a new fact, or a thought, or to record a portion of an emergency call.

The notebook became a place for certain types of information, unattributed fragments I wrote in from other texts, interspersed with my own thoughts and diary entries, as though by leaning into the fragmentation of my workday experience I might somehow conquer the sense of disarray and poor attention I felt daily on the phones.

And so I wrote down "Brewarrina" when the man called and shouted "Brewarrina". In his mouth the four syllables were compressed into something that sounded like Brwr-Na, but it made sense when I wrote it down. I asked him to clarify which state Brewarrina was in. There was only one. We both knew it. But I had to ask anyway.

Brwr-Na you stupid bitch can't you fuckin' spell hurry up I'm bleedin' to death.

Another important fact I learnt that year: when the body begins to panic the system floods with hormones. The panic enters the muscles, your nerves and your tissue proteins. It starts in the brain. The hypothalamus activates the sympathetic nervous system, which sends a cascade of adrenaline into your blood. Sight sharpens. Your heartbeat accelerates. Your breathing quickens. Your stomach ceases to digest. The airways in your lungs spread wide open. The blood races through your veins. Your emotions run riot. You might begin shaking. Glucose floods your internal grid like electricity during a power surge. Every cell of your being is set alight.

The panic response is so efficient that it has already taken full effect before the visual and intellectual centres of your brain have fully understood what is happening. It's why people jump out of the path of an oncoming car, turn and run from the encroaching fire, duck away from the drunken husband wielding the kitchen knife, before they even think about what they're doing.

The man from Brwr-Na stuttered on the phone as the ambulance connected through, his breathing staggered, his voice hoarse and moaning. Fuck, fuck, fuck, why aren't they answering?

I said, The ambulance will answer as soon as they can, and by the time I'd tried three different lines they still hadn't answered and he'd gone quiet, very quiet. As he whimpered, I'm fucking dying, I was looking up at the television where a smiling man was frying another egg on yet another stretch of suburban bitumen and when the ambulance answered the line was dead.

When it was over I stood up, logged out, and walked down the corridor to the bathroom. I shut myself in the stall and sat down on the closed lid. I focused on the white laminate of the

door and the advertisements stickered to the paint, a banana wearing a condom, a rape hotline, graffiti.

I recalled that in high school drama classes we would sometimes play games of "focus", in which the winner was the girl who could lie on the floor and stare at one place on the ceiling without giving in to the distractions of the other girls pulling faces and whispering dirty jokes above her. I always won. I acquired a reputation as "focused", but it occurred to me that afternoon in the bathrooms that what I felt on the floor staring at the ceiling was more like dissociation than focus. The faces and whispers were there, but I wasn't entirely certain that *I* was. The focus game was really just a kind of exercise in cleaving my mind from my body and floating away, with none of the "mindfulness" or "control" that the drama teacher pinned to my accomplishment when I was eventually invited to pull myself up from my prone position on the floor.

But I was good at it. And so I sat there, in the bathrooms outside the offices of Triple Zero on the first floor of a skyscraper on Elizabeth Street, focusing.

During my half-hour break, late that evening, a middle-aged man, a sculptor, read me Keats in the staffroom. He approached me, laughing before he'd even said what he wanted to say. He explained that I could punch him in the mouth if I preferred, but he wanted to read me some lines of Keats. They're pertinent to you, he said. He had the book open in his hands.

"She was a Gordian shape of dazzling hue," he began. "She seemed at once some penanced lady elf, some demon's mistress, or the demon's self... her head was serpent but, ah, bitter-sweet! She had a woman's mouth with all its pearls complete."

As he was reciting Maeve passed behind me as she made her way to the kettle. I felt her hand squeeze my shoulder.

*

Later, I found the poem, took a photograph of the stanza and sent it to Lachlan. I had by then reacquired a thirst for him. I think the thirst was what came to me initially, followed by affection. The first feeling I had for him was still bound up in those early conversations in the Woolley building when everything was possible and he was a Voice more than a man.

But the feeling gradually increased, because he was something that both aroused thirst and satisfied it, and someone too who seemed thirsty for me. I wanted, more and more, to be alone together, satisfying the thirst, forgetting about what had happened, and what was surely to come. It was not reasonable, but the things we want rarely are.

I walked home along Elizabeth Street at two in the morning with my keys wedged in between my fingers. Green trails of slime dripped down the sandstone walls of Central Station. There was nobody else out on the streets. I followed the lamp posts along the hot, dark stretch of Elizabeth Street, up the concrete staircase, to the front door and the second wooden staircase that led up to my bedroom. I locked the door and got into bed.

But I slept badly. The lights from the traffic and the Mascot-bound bus rotated across the walls in phosphorescent blue stripes. Two drunks screamed along the street. Ambulances and fire engines careened out of Cleveland Street all through the night, beelining a course into the south. I knew that each and every one of the ambulances and fire engines had been dispatched from phone calls put through by somebody I worked with, and knew that in a few hours I would be back there, in that office, summoning sirens. Before dawn the birds began to call. The house creaked. The room began to heat up. The sheets clung to my legs. The light crept across the floorboards in weak but insistent increments. I watched it move.

M Y FRIEND CLEMMIE stood in her kitchen chopping watermelon, dropping the slices into a plastic container as I explained that this was A Good Idea. This job thing, this plan I had devised. More and more I was living in the dark, aquatic place in my mind where such plans were defined only vaguely, by sentiments such as "leave" or "retreat" or, simply, "no".

Clemmie had known me longer and better than just about anybody. She and I had met the first day of high school. She found me pressed against a door frame picking at the starchy pleats in my new school skirt before our first class. She was already comfortable in the blue waistless thing, and she told me she liked my hair. She was a tall glowing thing that I envied as soon as I saw her. Even then, at twelve, there seemed something luxuriously wild about her. She smelled of Herbal Essences and yoghurt-covered muesli bars and liked to expose the blonde down on her shins, which she did not shave off until her second year of university.

That job sort of makes sense, Clemmie said. If you can hack it. I couldn't last at something like that. Just listening to all those people. People screaming and dying. I don't know how you aren't crying by the end of every shift. How long are you going to do it, do you think?

I don't know. Not long. The money is good. I've been able to save some already.

She looked at me sceptically and wiped the wet knife against her shorts. Beads of sweat rolled down the backs of her knees. So you're making yourself miserable for an indefinite period, for the sake of some cash? And for what?

I mean, I'm not miserable. I'm fine. I have time to write. But yeah, I'll have cash. If I'm careful. It seems like a good idea to get out of Sydney for a while. That's probably what I'll do.

That seems like a good idea. Like, if you're not happy here. Seems like all those friends you had from your course last year have fallen away. And the rest. The bad things. Well, *you* know what happened. You'd go to London, then?

Maybe London. Or America.

America? Clemmie turned and dropped the knife into the sink, along with the chopping board, pink and wet and fleshy as though she had just been butchering meat. Drops of watermelon juice dotted her toes and she bent down to wipe them with her hand. She thought for a second while she sucked the juice from the heel of her palm, then shook her head. London makes sense. But I can't see you in America.

"In the beginning all the world was America," said John Locke, long ago. A man who never set foot in the place, but believed in fresh starts. Only later, once my plans had come to pass, could I see that younger version of myself grasping for fresh starts like they were lifebuoys, and judging that America was the only one worth grasping for.

Five o'clock came. The southerly breeze began to insinuate itself through the wall of heat surrounding the city. The air glowing amber and thick with bushfire, we took the container of water-melon and a bottle of vodka and inched bare legs onto the hot leather surface of the seats of her car. We drove the back way through St Peters with the windows down. At Coogee we parked five blocks from the beach. We ran barefoot on burning asphalt down the steep hill past blocks of flats and scrubby bush, running through stalled traffic, long hair streaming over our shoulders,

along the sandy path by the barbecue pits and pines and the rippling grass and descending, at last, to the fine golden sand beyond which there was only water. The surface of the sand scorched the soles of my feet. We flung down towels and Clemmie stayed put while I ran. I jumped down the sandbank, running through the glistening bodies on their towels and into the waves.

I jolted to a stop. Taken aback. The rolling waves were, it occurred to me, the only boundary I could be certain of.

And even that boundary could be breached.

I swam out until I could no longer feel the ground beneath my feet. In the water, dipping and coming up again, I was swept for a moment into a sudden panic. I felt nothing below me and nothing to the sides. I was not afraid of the rip tide, of being pulled out. Yet I believed, in that instant, that there were snakes in the water, all around me. And the fear, given recent events, seemed entirely rational.

It had been like this since we were teenagers. Clemmie and I went to Coogee, to Maroubra, to Bronte, but never Bondi, and once we arrived the setup was always the same. While Clemmie tanned, I would swim out beyond the waves. She would watch me from the sand. Occasionally she would yell at me from her towel when I'd gone out too far. I would hear her voice—swim back!—pressing her untied bikini top to her small, flat breasts.

Looking back towards the shore now I could see her gesture for me to come closer. Swim back. The turning tide of early evening made her anxious. All that heat and beauty, like the beach was opening the velvet curtain and inviting you to gaze upon the tawdry lushness from which you might never want to turn away.

She had reason to be afraid that I would swim out too far, because I had done so before. When we were fourteen years old we had walked out into the waves at Bronte Beach. Both of us

had grown up swimming the city beaches. We knew that Bronte had rough surf, that the rips could be fierce, and that the flags always narrowly delineated the safe part of the beach. We knew how to handle ourselves in the water. Knew that you don't fight against a rip if you're caught in one. You have to surrender to the direction of the tide, swimming across it until you're free of the pull. But that afternoon when we were fourteen we had not paid attention to the tides. Clemmie followed me out, deep into the water. But then she began to panic. We're being pulled out to sea, she said. No we're not, I replied. But we can't touch the bottom anymore, she said. We were standing five minutes ago. She turned and began to swim back. Her strokes led her nowhere. No, I told her. Don't do that. You swim across the rip, remember, not against it. I acknowledged that we were caught in a rip, but I continued to tread water. I did not see any reason yet to be afraid. Clemmie flailed her arms. She called out. And then a lifeguard appeared on a jet ski, telling us to jump on. Oh no, I said, we're fine. You're caught in a rip, he shouted. Hop on, you're going to get pulled out. Clemmie hopped on, but I refused. I did not want to be rescued. Especially not by him. I believed that the water would treat me kindly.

Clemmie knew even then that it would not. She pulled me onto the jet ski and the lifeguard took us back to the shore. You always swim out too far, she said.

She didn't doubt that I knew my limits. She simply knew that I was more interested in crossing them than I ever was in staying safe.

Clemmie was forever making dramatic declarations and going back on them. Owning a pet was akin to slavery, she announced over gelato when we were fifteen. A month later she owned a guinea pig named Skywalker, which she kept in a cage in the back

49

garden. Piercings were an abuse of the body, she proclaimed on the platform of Strathfield Station, until she pierced her ears at twenty. Oral sex was disgusting because she did not like it, and on that I never heard her launch a counterclaim. When we were teenagers, I thought that she would wind up being the corrupt one, centre stage, while I looked on from my bookish place in the audience. She could flirt, she brought summer into a room on the tail of her big man's shirt, and I always thought she knew how to be in the world in a way that I didn't. But it turned out that, once I got around to it, I never thought oral sex was disgusting.

The year she first cast her assessment on oral sex, Clemmie had stopped sitting cross-legged on the ground with me on the city-bound platform of Strathfield Station after school. Instead she stood, leaning against a pole. My mother said that girls who sit on the ground have low self-esteem.

That's absurd, I told her, I'm not fucking standing.

For two weeks we waited for the train home, me sitting, Clemmie leaning against her pole, until eventually, and without acknowledgment, she wound up back on the ground with me, picking at the icing on stale strawberry doughnuts with her legs crossed. It occurred to me even then that I was, by dint of sheer stubbornness, forcing her down to my level.

As the sun dipped we wrapped ourselves in towels and bought hot chips from the kiosk. We walked north along the headland towards Bondi, past the sandstone bluffs and Gordon's Bay and the car park at Clovelly, up at last to Waverley Cemetery.

The warm breeze rustled the palm trees by the memorial to Irish sons killed in English wars. We walked towards the board-walk which rounded the cliffs and down towards the beach. A couple of tourists walked by, holding hands, squinting expectantly behind their sunglasses at the glimmer of Bondi ahead. There

were signs set up every few metres along the path, warning of unstable ground. The edges of the cemetery were crumbling. It sat upon a dyke filled with building waste, between two walls of rock. Below, the base of the cliff was being inundated with waves. It didn't drain properly. The land was breaking up piece by piece. In fifty years' time, once erosion and the rising waters had taken their toll, the cliffs would no longer exist. And who knew what would become of the bodies?

At the farthest outcrop of rock there was a lookout. I picked a flower from the bushes by the fence. Clemmie wandered ahead, looking north. I leant against the fence and turned, looking back towards the blood-red pulse of the light as it sank. From the edge of the ocean, it was easy see how seductive the west must have looked for those nineteenth-century men trapped at the edge of all this vastness, believing in the water that was Out There.

Back then, the British had believed an inland sea lay at the heart of Australia. They had stood right where I was standing on the edge of the continent and noted that some of the rivers didn't terminate down there in the churning ocean below the cliffs. Some rivers flowed west. Turned their backs on the Pacific and slouched suggestively inland.

In 1817 the colony's surveyor general, John Oxley, was sent out to explore and chart the Lachlan River. Dammed almost out of existence today, the Lachlan was a source of much excitement in the early years of the nineteenth century. It was one of those westward flowing rivers. Termination point unknown.

Oxley set out to trace the river's course, to see whether it led into the inland sea. The sea would make way for cities, farms, great feats of engineering, all the bounty of the empire. The inland sea was the landscape's logical promise for this scrap of

land in the far-right corner of His Majesty's maps. If there was no water in the interior, then what future could they possibly have in this country? Because the thing was, if you didn't believe in an inland sea and all that ripe promise of the landscape, you might then have to face what you'd done—set up home on this drought-ridden ancientness that you'd stolen and didn't understand. A land all dead grass and fire and pestilence. A ruined Eden you had convinced yourself, in some fever-dream, to stake a future on.

I had known about the inland sea my whole life, but during this final year in Sydney I began to think about it all the time. Because John Oxley was my great-great-great-great-grandfather. A descendant from my father's side, I had been told Oxley was somebody to be proud of. But I came to realize the story I had been told might not in fact be accurate. I began to think often of that feckless imperialist trudging through the landscape for all those weeks in 1817, slowly being overwhelmed by a sense of alarm that there was simply fuck-all Out There. No Providence, no Eden, no neat or rational conclusion to the narrative.

Except that wasn't what he reported when he got back to the coast. Oxley, our flesh and blood, was a consummate liar. A swindler and a fuck-up, whichever way you look at it.

Oxley failed to trace the course of the river, but he noted that the Lachlan did not stop flowing west. "I feel confident," he reported to the Governor upon his return to the coast, "we were in the immediate vicinity of an inland sea."

Why? Because he had smelt something like seaweed out there.

He had seen a swan fly across the horizon as he'd looked out across the flat salt plains that looked so seductively like the bottom of some long-ago seabed.

He hadn't seen the water.

But he believed in its promise.

I did not speak often to my father, but years ago, during a rare bout of affection, my father had sent me a copy of Oxley's journals. He included a letter with the book, explaining that he thought it important for me to appreciate our ancestral stake in History, and Empire. My father would, if challenged, earnestly forswear any allegiance to the atrocities committed by the Empire, but deep in his heart my father was proud of Oxley, had more admiration for him than for his own parents or children, for any prime minister or rock and roll guitarist. My father inflated the importance of Oxley's legacy so that it might overshadow any other aspect of our personal or national history.

I read the journals.

Here was what was in them: walking, heat, monotony. Men and desert and horses. A lot of talking about water.

"Nothing can be more melancholy and irksome than travelling over wilds, which nature seems to have condemned to perpetual loneliness and desolation," Oxley wrote. "We seemed indeed the sole living creatures in those vast deserts."

From the fence on the edge of Waverley Cemetery it was difficult to believe any place so beautiful could give way to the loneliness and desolation of the interior. Up ahead Clemmie held her phone down by her hips out of the glare of the sun, and the first flush of sunburn began to warm my shoulders. I turned my back on the west and looked down along the coast. There was something strange about the water heading south towards La Perouse. There were thin streams of algal bloom like slick oil or sewage spread out down the coastline. It was hard to be sure that it wasn't some dead or deadly thing coming into shore.

*

The word auspice refers at its root to the Roman belief that one could apprehend the future by tracking a bird in flight. The word describes a belief in the meaning of patterns, and encourages the human mind to read significance in, say, couches that have been pushed across front doors, in sea snakes in the water, in the progression of an algal bloom, in rivers flowing west, in the distant shape on the desert horizon that might be a swan.

If I had begun to consider leaving the city, it was here, in this muddle of auspices and water and lovers formed in the shape of failed rivers, that I now locate the source. Long afterwards it is easy to see the ways in which you thought you knew the story. You follow along the banks of the river and observe its course. But then the future falls apart at the seams. When the river trickles out into salt plains it's more than you can bear.

So, why, you begin to ask, should I not abandon this place? There is nothing left for me here. Just snakes in the water. Just sirens. Just phones ringing.

T HAT NIGHT a marginally famous actor was at the Courthouse. There had been a few years when you could expect to see him drinking every night in Newtown. The actor had put on weight and didn't look much like the man who had been on TV a few years earlier. Whenever I saw him he was drinking, and eyeing young women. I still thought he was handsome, and wanted to be one of the women he looked at, but even when he was tipsy and smiling in a corner of the beer garden there was something bitter about him that made it seem inadvisable to approach.

I pointed out the actor when Clemmie came back from the bar with a jug of beer. Her hair had dried from the beach into stiff waves. That guy again? she asked. I guess he hasn't been around as much lately, has he. She swept a finger across the spilled beer and brought it to her mouth.

Across the table from Clemmie sat two people I'd only met in passing once before. A woman with shiny hair, and her boyfriend, an underfed, nervy man whose name I had forgotten.

Maybe he got better, said the shiny-haired girl.

Nah, I don't think so, said the boyfriend. Friend of mine told me that the other week he was walking home after a night out. Passes by the BP in Erskineville. The one by the railway line. And that bloke was laying into some poor guy with a bunch of tattoos while his girlfriend stood to the side, just crying for him to stop.

The actor had punched the man with tattoos in the face five times, the boyfriend said. The man's jaw had cracked. His nose had smashed. Blood trickled into his eyes. And the actor, when he was done, had started half-apologizing, pacing, wringing his fist as though it hurt him. Then he stormed away from the BP while the tattooed man bled into the asphalt.

Guess he didn't get better then, I said.

Nup.

At midnight the Courthouse closed. We bought longnecks and bottles of bad white wine from the bar. Clemmie hid them in her bag before we caught the bus outside Newtown Station. She was too drunk to drive us to wherever we were going now.

The boyfriend of the girl with the shiny hair said these were good people. Friends of his, living in a building that had once been used to care for disabled children. The door opened, and a barefoot man ushered us down a dank corridor to what passed for a kitchen. The place was dark inside, with barbed wire over the windows. The ceilings were high, and unseen voices from other rooms echoed off the walls with the thump of the music. It was hard to say how many people were there, in the building, in all those abandoned rooms.

I walked along the hallway, approaching the thudding music. At the end of the building, an entryway opened into the source of the sound. One of the rooms had once been used for hydrotherapy, when the building still served its purpose. The swimming pool was smaller than average, and now that it had been emptied of water you could see the descending oblongs of space dug deeper into the concrete, until eventually even the tallest person would be totally submerged. The deepest part of the swimming pool was only a few feet long, and had been covered over with a blue tarp to form a kind of ceiling. From above, windows let in the light of the moon from outside. It was oddly peaceful, standing in that wide, empty space, all sounds echoing off the dry swimming pool tiles. I climbed down a ladder to get inside the empty pool. Below the surface, there were couches, bongs and a television

that was turned on but emitted nothing except a glowing purple light. Somebody had written the word "love" onto the screen with strips of gaffer tape.

You like it? asked one of the men sitting in the swimming pool.

Sure, I said. I was sitting on the sofa. The men snickered. There was a joke I wasn't in on.

I sat in silence on one of the sofas while the men passed a joint from hand to hand. I did not like the way that the television glowed, and the close smell of the space below the tarp. Nothing had ever been cleaned. I wondered why I did not just go home. Only it seemed that leaving would cause some sort of a fuss, and I did not want to seem rude, did not want to look like I couldn't hack it. Whatever this place was, it was meant to be fun, and I was meant to be enjoying myself.

A clattering above my head and a platform sandal on the ladder announced the descent of Clemmie into the swimming pool. The men looked up and followed her body as it stumbled towards me on the couch, handing me her beer for a sip and slinging her arm around me as though she were weightless. She was offered the joint and she took it.

When she turned to me she asked what was wrong. She observed that I was not being chill, and put her arm around me, as though her affection might make me more at ease in the sweet fug of marijuana and disquiet.

Hey, Clemmie asked, you want to hear something weird? The other day I got off the train at Marrickville and on the platform I found a wallet. It had some money in it, and the woman's licence and everything. So I took it to the police station, like, just walked it over there. And I guess it was Monday afternoon, so it was sort of a weird time of day. But I went to the police station and walked into the waiting room.

Waiting room?

Or whatever it is. It was so eerie. Because I stood there and stood there, but there was nobody behind the desk, and nobody came. It was just empty. And I started to get freaked out, because the door was open, I'd walked right in, but the longer I waited I started thinking how weird it would be, if the people that run the police had just up and left. Like, what would it be like if everyone who was meant to keep us safe, the city's protectors, what if they were just gone. No one to take the wallet from me, I could just go out and use the woman's money, there was no one to hand it to, no one to give it back to her. Just complete freedom to do whatever you wanted because there was no one to enforce the rules anymore.

They showed up though, right? Someone took the wallet from you.

Yeah. Took a long time though.

I've felt like that sometimes being at Triple Zero, especially the first week. When the police line takes a long time to connect through. Like, maybe there's nobody there in the police dispatch centre. Maybe they all just up and left. And I'm the only person left for whoever is on the phone freaking out. They freak out the longer the phone rings, and I keep telling them the police will answer as soon as they can, as though I know what the police are doing, but I don't really know. Literally the only thing I know is that the phone is ringing. Maybe one day they won't answer at all.

Yeah it's weird, huh?

We sat together in companionable silence, Clemmie gently combing my hair with her fingers. We were always touching one another, had been always, since we were twelve year olds. Picking leaves out of one another's hair, wiping away biscuit crumbs from skirts, smudging badly applied make-up on one another's cheeks.

I turned to her. Do you still walk home with your keys between your fingers?

Yeah, mostly.

Clemmie had told me, the year before, about the trick her ex-boyfriend had taught her. He had advised her that if you wanted to fuck somebody up, you could throw a punch with a key wedged between each of your fingers. He advised her to walk down the street at night like this, just in case.

I sort of do it automatically now, Clemmie said.

I've started doing it too.

Keys in your fist?

Yeah. When I have to walk home from work at night. Or on the bus. If it's late. And it's one of those eerie, empty night buses with just you and a stranger and the driver. I push the keys between my fingers and just hold on to them. I never used to do that, before I started working at Triple Zero. And it's only when I come home from work. I dunno, I wish I didn't. I wish I didn't know about all the bad things that could happen, didn't hear about them all day on the phones.

I think I started doing it when the woman died. In September last year I think it was? In Melbourne. Because I thought maybe if she had fought back then that man wouldn't have killed her.

She did fight back, I said, and pulled away from Clemmie. He was bigger and stronger than she was. She *did* fight back.

Did she? I dunno. It's scary, she said. You should quit that job.

No. I'm fine.

I stood up and shook my head. I'm going to get another drink, I said, and put a hand on her head as I left. The eyes of the men in the swimming pool followed me as I climbed up the ladder.

I had no intention of getting another drink. I simply wanted to leave without having to explain myself. It upset me to have her tell me that I was not cut out for my job, and it upset me to talk about the woman who had gone missing in Melbourne

the year before. *Leave, retreat, no,* my body compelled my brain, without any regard for social niceties.

I walked down a corridor and towards a door I thought might be the exit. Instead, the door led out into the garden where a shed was rotting into the grass. The garden appeared nearly empty, but I liked how overgrown it was. The moon that I had seen trapped in the glass of the hydrotherapy room was brighter out here, and seemed to fill the evening with light. Cicadas screeched in the trees, and for all the strangeness, I didn't mind, because it was cooler out there in the dark.

The only sign of activity was in the shed. Two men sat in the shadow of the open doorway, on plastic orange school chairs. They beckoned me over. Neither of them was wearing shoes. I was handed a beer.

You from around here? asked one of the men. I told him I lived in Redfern, and had grown up in Ashfield.

You don't talk much, do you? he said. I shrugged.

That's cool, he said. I like women who don't talk.

The stranger gestured to his lap, as though to suggest that I might like to sit there.

I F WE WERE TRULY RATIONAL, we would be deathly afraid of mosquitoes. After all, mosquitoes carry the sorts of diseases that, if you look at the sheer number of lives lost, make them just about the most dangerous insect on earth. I had always been told that cars were more dangerous than planes, and had never really taken the idea seriously, but the first weeks at Triple Zero taught me to reconsider their dangers.

Cars flipped over. They started smoking. They ran down children. They veered off the road, they smashed through houses in the middle of the night. They poisoned their passengers. I did not know how to drive, but if I had, I would have stopped. The calls made me walk along footpaths as far away from the road as I possibly could.

The fear of cars was joined by new, less rational fears—that the fuses would short and the house burn down, that the scaffolding over the footpath would collapse as I walked beneath it, that the waters would rise and swallow the street.

And so it seemed plausible to me that the Liverpool-bound train I was riding along the Inner West line could flip, that a body could launch itself in front of the metal as it sped along the tracks, that a man could fling open the door between carriages and rampage through the train with a knife.

On the seat behind me two blonde girls with dark roots commiserated with one another. He doesn't deserve you, one said to the other. That's what I told him! I told him he doesn't step up his game I'm out of there. I turned my phone black, rested my head against the glass and watched the houses slip by. I recited the stops to myself from memory, memories from childhood when the city seemed like a shimmering wonderland,

and memories from adolescence, when I took the train look-
ing always for something I never seemed to find. This stretch
of railway was the measure of how far I was, at any point,
from home. *Redfern, Macdonaldtown, Newtown, Stanmore, Petersham,
Lewisham, Summer Hill, Ashfield.* I counted down the stations as
they flew by.

I was on the train because my mother and stepfather were
gone for the week, and I had promised to feed the cat. I was
welcome to help myself to any food in their absence, and had
full licence to use both washing machine and dryer.

All the lights in the house were turned off except for the lamps
in the hallway and the front room, because my mother imagined
that such a strategy would prevent any potential burglar from
supposing the house was empty. I turned the hall lights on and
stacked the post on the hallway table and walked through to the
back of the house where I opened a tin of food and emptied it
into the bowl by the back door. There was no sign of the cat.
Probably hiding, or else dead from the heat. The news said that
January was of hottest-ever days and broken records, 123 by
the end of the season. Some days, the heat was so powerful that
people died simply sitting in their own homes. The newspapers
had started calling it the "Angry Summer".

I made tea. On the bench beside me sat a stack of papers
from the Saturday before they'd left. The crossword of the *Herald*,
filled out in two sets of handwriting. My stepfather's spiky con-
sonants against my mother's neat vowels. An eggy thumbprint
from the turning of a page. I opened the alcohol cabinet and
poured scotch into a glass, knowing that every year they were
gifted a new bottle, that they would barely miss it if I finished it.

As the light began to dim I took the glass and walked down
to the end of the house where the bedrooms were. I opened
the door at the top of the hallway and walked into my mother's

bedroom, where the bedside lights were turned on. I had been expressly forbidden to turn them off.

My mother kept all the photo albums on the top shelf of the wardrobe in her bedroom. There were maybe thirty of them. Putting the glass of whisky down on the bedside table beneath the lamp, I stood on the linen chest at the foot of the bed, opened the door and pulled down the albums at the very top of the stack. In those albums lived the few pictures there were of my parents and myself together.

In one photograph my father lay across the bed on the same paisley bedspread my mother still used. I lay beside him, sleeping, my hair knotty, my bottom in the air, face pink in sleep. In the photograph my father looked at me as though he could not quite comprehend what he was looking at. You couldn't tell anything about him from the photograph, not the Great Explorer whose blood ran in his veins, nor the harm he was capable of. Another photograph showed my father kneeling beside me while I reached out to pat a wallaby in Ku-ring-gai Chase National Park shortly before my father left Sydney and moved to Melbourne. "Darling don't you go and cut your hair," went the song on the radio from around the same time. When it played I remembered dancing with him in the basement where he kept the sound system. I was too small to really dance. I stood on his feet and we shuffled around the room. I could never remember the words to the rest of the song. But I took the idea of not cutting one's hair very seriously, particularly if you wanted men to keep calling you "darling".

Shortly after my mother and I moved into the house in Ashfield we were burgled. They had come into the room I was in right now, they had opened the wardrobe, they had taken the photo albums and the boxes and all of her clothes and they had thrown

them on the floor. They didn't destroy any of the photographs, only scattered them. Instead, the robbers stole the television, the stereo, my mother's earrings and my christening bracelet.

That night my mother had left work in the city, driven to pick me up from childcare and then taken us home. I remember that it was dark. She opened the corrugated-iron gate to park the car in the fibro shed we had in the garden then. We came in through the back. I walked ahead of her while she locked the back gate, through the garden and up the three steps to the veranda. I noticed in the dark that the back door was smashed through. There's broken glass, I said.

My mother pushed me back into the trees and told me to keep quiet. She crept into the house and I watched her move through the smashed-up rooms in her shoulder pads and high heels, looking and watching to see if whoever it was was still there. She squared her shoulders and kept her arms tight to her body. When she couldn't find anybody in the house she called the police. It was cold in the garden beneath the gum tree in the dark. I was not allowed into the house to see what had been done.

After the burglary, I sensed for the first time that the new house might not be safe. In the week after the robbery my mother had iron bars placed on all the windows, she had motion-sensor alarms fitted in the bedrooms, and a security screen added to the glass back door so that there would be no more broken glass. We had to leave the lights on when we went out, so that a passer-by would assume that somebody was home. But none of the measures she took to keep us safe made any difference when we came home alone at night. She held me behind her, ordered me to stand behind the rubber plant by the entryway, and she opened the door slowly. She disarmed the burglar alarm and entered the house on high alert. She would not turn on the lights until she was certain there was nobody there. Not until

I was a teenager was I allowed to walk into the house ahead of my mother, or to stop standing behind the plant. And even then, she was never easy. When I came home late she could never sleep, and sometimes she would call, or text. Be careful, she would say. Practise some responsibility.

After the burglary my mother never slept deeply again. In the middle of the night she would often wake up and I would find her half-dressed and peering through the slats of the plantation shutters into the street, looking for the prowler who had made the leaves rustle, the man with a knife edging up the side passage, the killer at the door.

Sometimes she was watching for a stranger. More often, I think now, she was waiting for my father.

I closed the pages of the album and opened the thinner folder at the bottom of the stack. As I pulled it onto my lap a large black and white image, maybe twenty-five centimetres wide, slid out of the pages.

The photograph showed a woman, very pale, with red hair, lying naked in a rich stretch of grass. The edges were white once, but yellow now. The photograph cut off just above the woman's nipples. Her breasts fell gently to the sides of her ribs, like mine. She looked away from the camera from the man who must have been standing directly over her, maybe lying on top of her, to take the picture. It was my mother, long before I had ever known her.

I had lived alone with my mother for years and seen her naked a thousand times, but it only occurred to me, looking at that photograph, that I looked like her. Had her breasts. And her hair. And an intensity of expression that, looking at the photograph of her stretched out on the grass all those decades ago, I realized had rendered her wholly and utterly vulnerable.

*

These are the ways in which I resemble my mother: blue eyes, red curly hair, same smile, same shape of nose and breast and forearm and fingernail, same sensitivity to various citrus fruits. A tendency towards intense feeling. A propensity for shouting. Terrible singing voices. We liked red wine and watermelon and rice pudding with sultanas. We were both, very often, fearful. She liked mangos, but I couldn't stand them. Every year at Christmas she bought a crate and ate them all herself. She was more cautious than I was. But it wasn't like I was any less afraid than my mother. I was afraid after the burglary, just like she was. If I wasn't interested in protection, it was because I didn't then see myself as something worth protecting.

One evening, when my mother and I were living with my grandparents, I had stood at the bedroom window in the dark. I was waiting for the arc of car headlights to turn in from the cul-de-sac and progress up the slope to the house.

I did not like to be left alone.

I can't remember how long I stood there in the dark, a tiny quivering figure of fury. I waited and waited, but the light didn't inch down the driveway. And then I saw the scissors on my grandmother's dressing table. The ones I was forbidden to touch. I took them in my hand, and stood at the bedroom window, snipping away at my curls as I waited. I could see myself reflected in the dark glass of the window, and it was immensely satisfying to see each strand of hair drop away as I cut it.

When I was done, a pile of curls lay in a mess all over the carpet.

And then the car headlights arced up the driveway. The door slammed. My mother entered the house. She progressed down the hallway. She turned the corner of the bedroom and she

saw me standing at the window and she saw my hair, and she screamed. What have you *done*? As though I had killed somebody dear to her.

She snatched up the curls on the floor and I had thought she was angry at me, I fully expected her to be angry, but the shock of the thing was when I realized that she wasn't shaking from fury. Down on her knees, my mother had begun to cry.

I'm sorry, I said to her, down there on the carpet. It was an accident.

But it had not been an accident. I looked at my mother as she scooped up the hair from the carpet. Before she had gone out I had sat on the bed while she changed, asking her questions, watching her struggle into underwear, the lovely flesh mapped with the straps and seams.

She was soft.

You should not harm a thing as soft as she was.

A week later I was taken to a professional hairdresser and given a new, shorter haircut to neaten out the mess I had made. But my mother was distant, something had changed in her demeanour, and even though I was a child I sensed that she had absorbed what I had done and taken it personally.

A week after I cut my hair, she gave me a book, *Safety First*. She explained that it was very dangerous for me to use scissors. I should never have picked them up. I could have caused myself an injury. As though my use of scissors was the real problem. She led me through the pages of the ex-library book, pages which explained all the things I could use to protect myself in bright, 1980s illustrations. "Everyone needs to be safe," the book began. "When you are safe, it means you are not in danger of being harmed." Safety pads and helmets, beware of open flames, stop signs and traffic lights, stranger danger, lock the doors, listen

to an adult and follow the rules. See, said my mother, this way nobody gets hurt.

It barely mattered. Safety first, or who got hurt, or why I had played with the scissors in the first place. It didn't matter. The scotch had made me drunk. Wavering and weepy. I fetched the bottle from the living room and took it back to the bedroom and set it down on the floor. I took up the photograph of my half-naked mother again. I took up the photo of my former self in Ku-Ring-Gai Chase National Park. The tears began to leak out of my eyes. I let them come.

Sometimes I drank just to have the sheer pleasure of weeping without apology, the luxurious, snotty weeping of childhood that can only be indulged, once you're grown-up, in the most solemn states of privacy. I lay back on my mother's bed and wept briefly for the voices on the phones. And then a deeper, more expansive weeping for all my former selves in all the photographs splayed across the paisley bedspread. The baby with the father whose nature and temperament she couldn't comprehend. Then, for the child who wanted more than anything to touch whatever creature would allow her touching. Then, the teenage girl who believed in the romance of all the poems she read, a girl too shy to ever talk about them with another flesh-and-blood person who could have helped make her happy. And then finally, with perverse pleasure, for the woman of the year before. For the events that had ushered in this splendid conflagration of emergency.

S IX MONTHS EARLIER.

It began the way it always does. I pulled my underwear down and there was no blood.

But there were cramps, and that was what caused me confusion. The cramps gave me conviction in the logical outcome. During a break before a meeting with my thesis advisor I walked to the other side of campus where I bought extra-strength ibuprofen from the university chemist, and for four nights in a row I took the pills before I went to sleep. Because I had cramps, and I was certain that the bleeding was imminent, and that the pain would come in the middle of the night. I was being "responsible", and taking steps to manage the pain. But in the mornings nothing had changed. The cramps were still there but the blood didn't come.

I looked up the symptoms of pregnancy on my laptop on a Tuesday morning. I felt queasy. That was a sign. So was the pain. Cramps indicate that the uterus is contracting to accommodate a foetus. Many of the early symptoms of pregnancy were also symptoms of period pain. I took painkillers and waited.

But the blood didn't come.

When you buy a pregnancy test the box comes with a set of two, just to make sure, and so it happened that in the bottom of my bedside table, I had a spare. I had been through this before. And it had been nothing. Just a hormonal reaction to stress. What could be more reasonable? I sat on my bed focusing on the absence beneath the fireplace until I felt quite dissociated from my body. Only then did I take the box downstairs to the bathroom.

69

I peed on the stick and laid it flat and results-down on the bathroom tiles as instructed. The intractable orange mould was climbing the edges of the bathtub. The sound of the buses accelerating leaked through the open window, a dog barking, the theme music to *Buffy the Vampire Slayer* playing in somebody's living room. I flipped over the test. To the two pink lines. I noticed that the breeze through the open window was quite cold. No, I told the two pink lines of the test in my lap. No.

And then I called the office of the university medical services.

On the morning of the appointment I woke to the blue wash of dawn in a bed not my own. Lachlan was asleep, snoring softly with his back to me. I watched his flesh rise. And fall. The books on the shelves. Outside I could hear the early din of birds waking up in the paperbark tree. The voices of construction workers arriving at the house under renovation next door and slamming the doors of a van. I looked at his back, and I thought about what it might be like to skip the appointment, and stay with him, naked, all day. It was so tempting. We could stay with one another forever in that bed, and we would be safe.

I put a hand to my stomach then. The skin and softness of it. And the dark knot inside me with which I had been communing all week. This fulcrum that decided whole futures. This thing which had narrowed and sharpened every moment since I'd learnt of it. This thing that was mine. And he was sleeping through it.

I watched his back rise and fall.

I peeled away the blankets and stepped into the freezing cold of his bedroom, as quiet as I could be. I didn't want him to see me leave. I was afraid that if he woke up he would say goodbye, and roll over to check his phone. I was afraid that he wouldn't offer to come with me. I wanted my mother.

I watched my blue reflection in the mirror of his wardrobe door as I dressed. The framed photograph of Patrick White glowered down from the wall. I wrote Lachlan a note on a piece of paper and left it beside him, in bed, in the space where my body had been. I shut the door and descended the stairs. My head hurt, and I was thirsty. But I wasn't meant to eat or drink anything beforehand.

I walked to the station under a canopy of magpies screeching at me from the trees. I took the train home to change. The carriages were quiet and unpeopled. Rush hour hadn't yet begun. At home, I showered him off me. I was thirsty.

The clinic to which the doctor at the university health service had referred me was unmarked and halfway up Devonshire Street, not far from Central Station. An entryway screened by ferns and opaque windows shielded the door of the clinic from view of the street. It was painted a pale green, and I wondered whether they had painted it that way because they believed that pale green was a soothing colour. I had walked past the building a hundred times and never noticed it before.

The receptionist was British, and that seemed reassuring. I handed her my Medicare card and my credit card through the gap beneath the bulletproof glass. She told me to have a seat in the waiting room. The chairs along the walls were lined with thick purple upholstery, more office decor than medical. A television mounted on the wall close to the ceiling played an episode of *30 Rock*. On the other side of the room two men sat waiting alone. There was only one other woman, a scrawny girl in a purple velour tracksuit accompanied by a heavyset Filipino man with acne-pitted cheeks. I looked at their faces but I couldn't detect any emotions. For a moment I could believe the waiting room was the kind of place with no particular purpose. It was simply a space to sit alone on purple chairs, watching *30 Rock*.

I sat focusing on the television ahead of me but focus was not a state I could achieve. I thought about the book my mother had given me when I was a child. *Safety First.* Beware of open flames, do not approach the floodwaters, don't struggle in the event that somebody tries to prevent your drowning. It was a book full of all the ways to protect yourself. But I supposed I had neglected most of the warnings, because I was not very good, on reflection, at keeping myself safe.

The receptionist behind the bulletproof glass had told me I would not be able to get home on my own after the procedure, and I had told her I would manage. I typed out a message. I'm scared, it said. I clutched my phone in my fist, just waiting for it to illuminate itself with his name. But he did not reply.

The receptionist called my last name. I was led through two heavy doors and down a corridor to a room where I was instructed to sit across the desk from the doctor. The walls were the same pale green as the exterior of the building. I could not look the doctor in the eye, and she seemed comfortable with that. She was plump. Her curly hair was turning white. She read from a piece of paper clamped to a manila folder.

Eight weeks, I told her. The father knows, I told her. I'm twenty-two, I can't do it. She filled out the paperwork, ticking the boxes and signing off at the bottom of the page.

She asked me if I was sure, and I said yes, because I was. There was nothing else to say.

A nurse led me into the belly of the building. She left me in a room to take my tights off and gave me a medical gown to cover the rest of me. It was cold in the small green room. No windows. I would not need to take my jumper off, the nurse had said. I pulled my tights down and laid them on a chair. The skin of my legs was pale, resistless. I observed thumb-shaped bruises on my thighs. I held myself very tense and very still, sitting on the chair, in the silence.

The nurse returned. She took my blood pressure and weighed me and listened to my breathing. Then I sat on the chair in the small room where she'd left me. I watched my bare legs swinging. They did not touch the ground. I had no underpants on but I clutched the spare pair in my hand. They had told me to bring a spare pair. It occurred to me that I had never worn a medical gown before, and I wondered what it would feel like, this thing that I was about to do. I wondered if it would hurt.

My heartbeat made green shapes on the monitor. Rising and falling. A beeping. The clamp on my finger. Three figures moving above me. Somebody placed my feet in metal stirrups. Legs spread. The swell of anaesthetic before the black.

Count backwards from five, honey.

Five, four, th—

I was gone.

A ND WAS SNATCHED through time into pain. Alone and wordless and clutching at the orange juice offered by a nurse, and searching for some sort of comfort in the fluorescent lighting and antiseptic of the room in which I'd woken. They lifted me into a seated position and told me to keep my blood sugar up. I set my eyes on my lap, but I didn't see myself or my body, only the pale green atrocity of the hospital gown.

I became aware of a sound that I discovered was being issued from me.

A howl.

Full of a grief I could not describe or examine, could not put words to, or name, I cried. Behind the curtain. Alone. For the first time. For my. For the thing I had lost.

FLOOD

THE PRESSURE GOT LOW. In the north of the continent the clouds gathered, spun and began to take form. The rain came down and swept over the tropics, tearing up everything in its path. Lounge furniture in trees, downed power lines, crocodiles on the median strip. Borroloola first, then Kowanyama, a pirouette over the Gulf of Carpentaria, and then a monsoonal flow that sent it tearing down along the Pacific coast towards the cities. The storm rumbled through the north—dark, wild shapes that came in and out of focus on the horizon like a lover met once in a dream. To be on the safe side, the Queensland Premier ordered the pre-emptive release of water from the Wivenhoe Dam.

But it didn't matter much when the waters got wild. The rivers peaked. The levees breached. Water spilled over the banks of the Burnett and the Logan and the Mary, all the capillaries in the suicidal region's veins, now opened. Bundaberg evacuated, Kogan and Tara cut off. Landslides on the Burnett Highway. A state of emergency stretching all the way down to Brisbane and heading south. Helicopters flew over the roofs, and gum trees peeked out from the roiling, snake-infested waters. They plucked the lucky few from the rooftops. By the time the floods reached Brisbane the Premier warned the state that the city's water treatment plant would need to be shut down. He advised his citizens to conserve their liquids. It was rumoured that some parts of the city would run out of drinking water within three days. As the flood swept south across the state line and into New South Wales all the records were broken. A thousand-year flood, again, when there had been a thousand-year flood only three years earlier. How high could the waters possibly rise? How heavy the rain?

Some hideous auspice, this, or proof of God's displeasure, or else just simply bad luck. The Prime Minister conceded that it was indeed "a tough period".

And so the waters crept. The ocean bled into the land. Salt water seeped into the crops. Rivers not rivers. Homes not homes.

Two bodies recovered from the waters near Burnett Heads were found bloated and rotting and were described as difficult to identify. A three-year-old boy was hit by a falling tree at Gordon Park and died. Elsewhere, a man drowned when he was swept away by floodwaters in the Oxley Creek. The Oxley Creek, named in honour of my ancestor, who stoked the fever of belief in like-minded men, the belief that out there in the continent there was water, and that the water would save us all.

I HAD BY THEN stopped seeing many people outside the hours of work. Maeve and Clemmie were my closest friends, but I kept them at arm's length. That summer, every source of comfort felt potentially threatening. When I picked up my phone and typed out messages to Lachlan it was with all the desperation of reaching out for a drug you thought you'd once renounced.

But I was not lonely for company. I spent time with plenty of strangers.

I had discovered, during the summer, that sex came quite easily. There was a friend of Maeve's boyfriend who still lived at home and snuck me in past his sleeping parents' bedroom door. There was a man whose name might have been Jonathan who I met at Kelly's at three in the morning. There was a man with a slicked-back pompadour who lived in Enmore. I slept with him every week for a month, and then when I got bored I slept with his best friend. There was a guy from Maroubra grinding his teeth on MDMA. There was a man who followed me through the beer court and down the long bathroom corridor at the Marly. There was a filmmaker from Melbourne who texted when he was in town. There was somebody I met at a party in Leichhardt whose name is lost to me forever. He broke into a car and went down on me in the back seat.

It was possible, I had come to realize, to be touched every night of the week by a different man if I wanted to be. As long as I didn't say much and I looked OK, there was always somebody that would have me. And I wanted to be had. By many. It didn't matter who. Take your shirt off, babe, and Good girl, and Let me see you touch it, and Close your eyes. They all merged together, and I didn't close my eyes, didn't want to, even when it stung.

When I thought of the men I saw them assembled as statues in a long gallery. I was fucking my way towards something serious in that silent, marbled place. I was accumulating bodies.

Most often, these were the sorts of men who, if I had been interested in avoiding men it was clear it was best to avoid, I would not have gone near. They had a kind of eroded beauty to them. Rough. Older. Hair growing on their shoulders and chests and backs. Acid had eaten into the bronze of their features. They had scars, raised veins and faded tattoos. But none of that mattered, and I wasn't afraid to approach them.

I wanted to be undone. I wasn't interested in protecting myself. And, besides, none of them affected me for longer than it took for the hangovers to fade. And so it didn't matter what I did with them during the nights I went to find them, and it didn't matter what I let them do to me.

In February, one of these men, Mark, pressed me up against the wrought-iron railings outside a party in Centennial Park held for an obese white rapper from New York who was then touring the country. I had been invited to the party because Maeve's boyfriend thought they needed more women. Across the road from the house, against the viridescent darkness of the park, Mark had kneaded my breasts while the railings dug into my spine. This is unreal, he said, again and again until the word "unreal" ceased to have any meaning. As though he had not touched breasts in some time.

Mark had brown hair flecked with grey. He was a full decade older than I was, and about to move to the Northern Territory to work as a social worker on an indigenous settlement. The night in Centennial Park would be his last weekend in the city, and so I agreed to see him in Coogee the following evening.

I met him beneath the pines along the waterfront. The air rushed up from the beach and out on the water the surfers

bobbed gently on the waves, clocking the breakers. Seaweed was tangled along the sand.

He told me he had an idea of where to take me. I used to come out here when I was a teenager and smoke, he said. It's like a small piece of wilderness in the middle of the city.

We headed north along the coastal path, around the cliffs. He led me towards a fence hung with a sign that advised you to beware of uneven terrain. We jumped it, and walked along a sandy trail through wild grass and bush until we came clear out onto a sandstone bluff overhanging the rim of the Pacific. We climbed down to a lower terrace so that the cliffs formed a shelter around us. Below, the sea surged against the rocks. He laid down a picnic rug and I took off my shoes. He brought out bottles of beer from his bag as I leant forward to watch the water surge below.

Earlier that morning a woman hiding behind a closed bedroom door in the Northern Territory had called. She whispered, My husband, he has a knife, he's trying to hurt me. I'm hiding beneath the bed please come quickly. And her voice broke as I asked her where she was. Darwin. Fannie Bay, she whispered, Northern Territory. Shit, I can hear him coming down the hallway please hurry. The police answered, she began to scream, I read out the job number over her cries and hung up as the phone made the clattering sounds it does when it falls out of a hand.

But I did not mention the call, or the fact that it was all I could think about as he told me about his impending move to the Northern Territory. I had learnt by then that it was best to keep such connections to myself. Instead I listened while he told me about growing up on these beaches, the spiritual retreat down the coast he had just returned from, the drive back through bushland all ashen and white from the fires that had burned through a month earlier.

I could remember how bushland looked when it was ashen like that. The fires of '94 had burned out the land around the house where I once lived with my parents. Those weeks were the first in living memory when fires had entered the city itself. When Sydney was threatened by total isolation, all the roads closed, cut off on all sides by the flames, when ash rained down and the sun turned red and we lived under orange skies. Even now I could remember driving through Ku-ring-gai National Park, three weeks after the fires had burned out, nothing in sight but blackened branches raised up, as though they were trying to clutch at something just out of reach. My mother had explained that the fire didn't kill the bushland, that nothing was dead, although dead was how it looked.

Because the country had evolved to burn. The seedpods of the banksia and the bottlebrush could only open in the intense heat of the fires, could only spread their seeds in scorched earth. The bush needed to self-immolate once in a while, and a catastrophic wildfire was par for the course, was in fact *necessary*. I remember looking out through the windows at the burnt trees and thinking I had never seen anything so impenetrable and beyond my ability to understand. And I thought, not that I could die out there in that landscape if I was cast out into it, but that disappearing would be so easy. That the disappearing would be the temptation.

Mark smiled. Yeah, I used to go up to Ku-ring-gai a lot as a kid too.

I nodded. I sipped my drink. I didn't think that had been my point.

Below the water surged against the rocks. I noted that this place was absolutely not a wilderness, as he had promised. It was a stretch of bushland along a cliff face in the middle of the city. Planes flew into Kingsford Smith overhead. Container ships

82

progressed along the horizon. From the cliffs I could see south along to the Coogee headland and, turning my head, the mouth of Gordon's Bay. I thought of the sea snake from the beginning of the summer, but I did not mention that either.

We drank the beers, and watched the water. When he kissed me, he laid me down on the rug so that my head lay right at the edge of the cliff face. He undressed me without my being quite conscious of it, so that in the end I was lying on the rock naked but for my bra.

Is it safe here? I asked.

Yeah, of course. It's fine. I'll protect you.

What if there are snakes?

There aren't, don't worry.

His breath roared in my ear, the rasp of belly hair against my skin. The longer he moved inside me, the more I felt my body being pushed to the edge of the cliff, the louder the waves crashed on the rocks below. I pressed the small of my back flat to the ground, I gripped one hand against the sandstone, the wind took a lock of hair and it went over the edge, but I did not.

Later, when the sky turned dark, we had sex again in the car park at Clovelly Beach, in the back seat, sitting up and facing the rippling sea through the windscreen. Mark was worried afterwards, because it was his parents' car and the upholstery smelt like semen. We lingered in the car park for fifteen minutes with all the doors wide open, to air it out in the breeze.

I F I WAS AFRAID of snakes on the cliff, I put it down to the reptile exhibit.

Not long after our house was burgled when I was four, my mother strapped me into the front seat of the car and drove us across the city, down Anzac Parade, to the termination of the loop at La Perouse. It was a Sunday afternoon, and this drive was meant to be "a treat".

We parked by the edge of the headland, got out, and walked towards a rust-coloured corrugated-iron fence with a rainbow serpent painted on its side. People were already beginning to congregate around the fence. A yellow hand-painted sign stuck up by the railing read Cann Brothers Reptile Exhibit. The light was dipping west over the snakepit.

In 1909, the snake men set up at a pit at the termination of the tram loop at La Perouse where the Pacific eases into Botany Bay. In the pit, the family's collection of lizards and snakes crawled and reared and sometimes lunged open-mouthed at the men's leathery skin. The snake show had happened every Sunday, every year, with different men.

The Snake Man entered the pit and the crowd applauded. Old-timey music played over a crackling sound system. The old man wore a baseball cap and long pants. Children hung over the sides of the fence. Tourists clicked the buttons on the black cameras slung around their necks.

The man had five large burlap sacks and a long stick with a hook in his hand. The burlap squirmed. One by one he loosened the openings of the sacks and the snakes dropped out. A little boy next to me smeared a rainbow Paddlepop into his gaping mouth. The snakes reared up on release and writhed across the

pit. I was pressed against the fence, my mother behind me. The Snake Man took some of the lizards and a python, offering them up for us to touch. The Paddlepop boy and I held out our fingers to stroke the reptiles like we were petting a cat. The scales were cold, and hard, and I didn't mind the lizards but I did not want to touch the snakes. My mother pushed me from behind, urged me to stroke its scales. But I wouldn't, and he moved on, back to the squirming sacks.

The Snake Man pointed to the painting of the rainbow serpent on the corrugated iron. He explained, for the benefit of the tourists, that the rainbow serpent had a special significance to Australia's first people. The snake was the creator god, but, like other ancient gods, the serpent was sometimes angry, and vengeful, and acted without mercy. Sometimes, the snake could be an omen of danger. He would avenge the land and punish those who had trespassed upon it.

Now, people can be scared of snakes, the Snake Man said, but more people die in this country by getting hit by lightning than from a snake bite. Because, see, what's remarkable about Australian snakes is how few people they bite given how venomous they are.

He picked up a long, copper-coloured snake, the size of a woman's ankle. He held it so that its mouth gaped open. See, he said, pointing at its teeth. When they bite it's nearly always self-defence. And they inject venom only about half the time.

He pointed to the fangs from which the venom would come. The fangs that would fold flat down against the roof of the mouth until the sensor under its nose detected the presence of a hot body, until a footfall caused the earth beneath its belly to tremble. All these sensations might impinge upon the creature's safety and cause its fangs to come out.

Snakes are not cruel, the Snake Man insisted. They never attack their own kind. But such a thought was not helpful. Because what do you do once the venom enters the bloodstream? Apply ice, or don't. Compress, or don't. Clutch a rosary, employ sacred herbs, recite a prayer. While the venom spreads and the pain comes and the muscles begin to spasm and the tissue breaks down and there is nothing you can do to halt it. What then does it matter whether it was an act of cruelty or otherwise?

Now these ones here are dangerous, very, very deadly, the Snake Man noted as he emptied a brown snake onto the yellow grass. The snake made towards me at the edge of the corrugated-iron fence, its body rippling and rolling across the dead grass. Come here, you, the man said, and drew its body back with the hook on the long metal pole. The snake reared up as though it were about to strike. The Snake Man continued to commentate: This one's pretty quiet. Now, a fierce snake wouldn't be standing up like that. If he was fierce he'd be straight on my leg before I knew what was going on, and when they strike they strike with their mouths open.

I stared at the open mouth of the snake. The horror was all so simple, even then. The eroticism of snakebite, the act of penetration, all those Freudian fears of the phallus, of being swallowed whole, the uncanniness of a creature that can shed its skin when we so often long to be able to escape our own. We are scared to death not of actual snakes but the snakes that live in our minds.

But understanding the fear doesn't make it any less real. If the snake show at La Perouse was meant to convince me of the hollowness of our fears, it failed. From that afternoon I was afraid of snakes more than just about anything else. Snakes in the long grass by the highway. Snakes hidden in the woodpile. Snakes in the water the worst kind, because the water was where I felt safe.

When the show was over my mother led me across the grass to look out to the water and the old military fortifications on the edge of the headland. That man, she said, has been there since I was a little girl. And it was his father before him. Your nana brought me here to see the same show when I was small.

What happened to the man's dad?

Died of snakebite, the idiot. They're a pack of idiots, those men. Think they're immune to all the venom because they've been bitten so many times. But it'll be snakes that kill every single one of them.

I stood there looking at the waves coming in across Botany Bay. The thorny bushes below pushed up against the shore. *When they strike they strike with their mouths open.* I asked my mother whether there were snakes down there, along the water's edge. Maybe, she said, but they don't *want* to hurt you. And then reached for my hair to smooth a curl, because my hair, she said, was my most important feature.

My mother was always playing with my hair. Always trying to smooth it down. She was always coming at me with her hands to try to "fix" whatever she found unruly about it, in much the same way that she would observe the things I did which, she was quick to inform me, she would never do.

T HE SUMMER CARRIED ON. There were fires in Tasmania, and along the eastern seaboard the heat did not abate so much as level out at a temperature just below unbearable. By the end of February only six million dollars had been raised for the Queensland flood appeal. Emergency costs alone were expected to exceed twenty-five million.

By then, the three women who I had been hired with in that office on Market Street had all been fired. They couldn't, in the end, spell the names of the tricky towns. Couldn't reliably answer the phone within three seconds. The girl with the dark roots cried at her desk. But I stuck it out. I looked like I could hack it. I wrote things down in the notebook when I felt overwhelmed.

For instance:

St Augustine believed a Flood was warranted every once in a while. God would always save the good. Only the wicked would be hurt. By Augustine's logic, in the story of the Flood, it was the people who were killed in the deluge, not God, who were responsible for the catastrophe. They fucked up, accumulated an unseemly number of sins, and so they were punished. Augustine called the thousand-year storms of climate disaster "natural evils".

After months at sea, Noah released a bird from the ark, which flew out across the floodwaters to see if they had abated. The bird did not return. And so they knew the worst had passed and the world could be rebuilt. This single act has led a great number of people, including my great-great-great-great-grandfather, to put their faith in the questionable symbolism of birds.

*

When I was at work, the hours seemed to spread outwards, shifts taking on the weight of weeks as I watched the overhead clock blink down the minutes remaining until I could leave. I watched the midday movie in silence and the six o'clock news on Channel Nine. When a call appeared on the screen, I pressed enter, and listened—to a man whose friend had been pulled out of their car at the traffic lights and was being beaten on the side of the road. To a girl who was so drunk that she didn't know how to get home. To a woman, in a town so distant that there was no phone reception, explain that she had happened upon a little boy on the highway in the middle of the desert, whose father had left him out there to die, and driven away in the high-noon heat. In the notebook beside me I wrote down "heat". I wrote down "desert". I wrote down "crying".

In this manner the days arranged themselves into something like routine. I worked four days a week, sometimes three. I had money enough to pay my rent. If it sometimes felt like the emergencies of those on the phones were leaking through the borders of my own personal emergencies, I had at least developed reliable habits. I took to wearing flowers in my hair. I swam when I could. I kept the windows open at night so that the bedroom sometimes seemed a mere extension of the mulberry, fig and mango trees that grew on the ledge between the houses and the street.

When I returned home the most I could usually do was lie in bed, reading. I had taken to keeping bottles of wine atop one of the bookcases, as well as a glass, and there were few nights when I did not fall asleep with a purple stain on my lips. If I had time in the mornings I wrote, although I did that in bed as well, for I had not thought to buy a desk. I had some writing assignments coming through, and in one month I managed to write four long pieces for a website. The editor of the literary

magazine had emailed asking if I was interested in some unpaid editorial work on top of the interviews I had agreed to conduct. I accepted. The website paid me one hundred dollars per submission, sometimes double, and even with the unpaid writing work at the literary magazine I was beginning to slowly save up money, enough money for a plane ticket.

L ACHLAN LIVED in a terrace house in Erskineville with two other men. The paint peeled away from the plaster walls, mould grew in their bathroom as it did in mine, and *Women's Weekly* cookbooks from the 1960s were piled on top of the kitchen cabinets, although nobody was sure where they'd come from. The rent was cheap because the toilet was still at the back of the garden. Walking down the path I tried not to brush against the oleander overgrowing the backyard. When I sat down to pee in the middle of the night I could see the stars through the gap between the roof and the corrugated-iron door. Spiders lived in there.

I walked back along the path and took a seat on a milk crate in the back passage where Lachlan and his housemate Sean were smoking.

Sean had moved in over the summer, in the months when Lachlan and I had stopped speaking. I had known Sean in my first year at the university, but we had fallen out of touch. Back then, he and I had got into the habit of meeting every Tuesday afternoon at a café on Glebe Point Road to read one another's writing. Sean had discovered the novels of Anaïs Nin. Erotica, he remarked once, is very interesting. At the end of semester he gave me a story to read in which a man walks into an empty church and has sex with a corpse. The woman, who he had never possessed in life, was laid out on the altar, having died some gentle, non-specific death. However she had died, it hadn't ruined her body. It wasn't suicide from a bridge, which would have liquefied her limbs, or a long drowning which would have bloated her immaculate flesh. She was just a pretty girl, laid out in an empty church, and the narrator was there to fuck her. We

didn't see much of one another after that. Whenever I went to see Lachlan at his house and saw Sean now, sitting in the living room, I felt a physical repulsion. I could not talk to him without picturing the imaginary dead girl in the church of his head.

Lachlan knew I didn't like him. Couldn't stand to listen to Sean sermonize, at that moment, on Fanon. "Every citizen of a nation is responsible for the actions committed in the name of that nation," he quoted at me, and I didn't disagree, I just didn't want to be told what I already knew to be self-evident. I stood up and walked into the living room to look for a bottle of wine.

Cate was in there, sitting on the sofa. Oh, I've been meaning to talk to you, she said. Come sit with me. I haven't seen you in so long, I've missed you.

This struck me as insincere, given that we had never been friends, only friendly.

That week in Sappho Books on Glebe Point Road I had seen a flyer for an experimental poetry reading, with her name included in the line-up. But Cate was the sort of person who had no addictions—she did not so much as drink coffee—and this seemed to me to imply a level of fortitude and self-reliance that was unreasonable in a poet. Her fingernails were very clean.

I had seen Cate's bedroom once, the year before when we were in Honours seminars together and she had organized a dinner party. Then, I had noted that she had cherry-print shoes in her wardrobe and prints of Degas's ballerinas on her wall and prizes awarded by Pymble Ladies' College still pinned to the corkboard above her desk. She never drank too much or stayed out too late or did anything to disgrace herself. I could not take her seriously as an experimental poet. She was a girl from a world of rhododendrons and cul-de-sacs and golf club memberships. Everything about her manner and her comportment

in Lachlan's unclean living room in Erskineville indicated that she was inhibiting more conservative impulses.

That night in Erskineville, when she asked me to sit beside her, I thought she was being cruel to me. I thought she was speaking with all the false sincerity of the North Shore private-school girl she had once been, a false sincerity with which I was all too familiar because I had been a private-school girl of the Inner West. I assumed Cate knew everything that had happened six months earlier, and that she pitied me. Now I understand that, in relations between her and me, Cate was never the cruel one.

I sat beside her and balanced a mug of red wine on my knee. The men sat together in the back passage, smoking, and I wanted to be out there with them, instead of inside, on the sofas, with no cigarettes.

A naked bulb hung from the ceiling. It swayed in the breeze with the windows opened, and it made the shadows swing with it. Somebody had thrown something brown or yellow against the wall. The colour had dripped and hardened, drying in rivulets towards the floorboards. There was a crack in the wall below the staircase across the room. Years ago, somebody must have tried to seal it up with Spakfilla. Now it was crumbling, pockmarking the plaster, a whiter wound in the wall itself. The staircase led up to Lachlan's bedroom. Cate's things were up there. It was for her that he had ended things with me, for her he had wanted to be a good man. *Good*. With her clean fingernails and empty hands I understood that she was precisely the sort of girl men might want to be good for.

Through the open window that let out into the outside passage where the men were smoking I heard Sean hold forth. Lachlan looked up. Our eyes met down the length of the passage. He was sitting on the red milk crate, smoking in silence. He looked at me sometimes, down the passageway. And then I could see it.

His face. Saying it and then unsaying it. Wanting the thing that he saw when he looked at me.

On the table where I rested my wine sat a splayed copy of *The Tree of Man*, dog-eared, plastered with Post-it notes. *The Tree of Man*, originally titled *A Life Sentence on Earth*, was written with "no plot, except the only one of living and dying". It was my favourite of White's books. The novel's female character is possessed of all the jealousy and restlessness of her author. She seduces and is seduced. "It is quite possible to be consumed by love for one individual," wrote White, "and to be led to a fatal wallowing in something else at some point in one's life. A kind of desecration of the noble ideal one can't attain to." Lachlan was not, so far as I know, writing his dissertation on love or wallowing or dashed ideals. I cannot recall precisely now, but I think he was writing on modernism and style and rhetorical subjectivity.

Cate had made herself hot chocolate. She clutched it between her hands. The mug, which was hers, looked cleaner than any other crockery I'd seen before in the house. Her face turned solemn as she sat. She put her hand on my arm. How have you been? You've not been around for months. I was beginning to worry. Have you been having a bad time of it?

I shrugged, and looked down at her hand on my arm.

I'm glad you're here, she said.

As we sat there together in the living room of Lachlan's house in Erskineville, I remembered, quite suddenly, travelling on a late-night bus from London to Paris through the Channel Tunnel when I was eighteen. The roads were slick with rain, shining in the headlights as the bus drove southwards. A girl sat in the seat in front of me. I couldn't see her face, only that she had not taken off her coat and that she was probably not a lot older than I was. She had taken a phone call as we pulled out

94

of Victoria, speaking in quiet, clear French to the person on the other line. After that she sat quite still as we sped along the M20. She had no book, and no headphones. And then, as we got closer to Dover, I realized that she was crying. The crying progressed quite rapidly into sobbing, her shoulders shaking and beginning to spasm against the window. Her hair hung down so that her face was hidden. The bus was nearly empty and she was smothering the sounds. I was the only person who might have noticed her. And I did nothing. Had no clue if I should. I watched her sob until her heavy breathing turned into exhaustion, and finally she fell asleep. She slept all the way through the Channel Tunnel and into the ugly concrete outskirts of Paris. And I was paralysed. I did not know what had happened or how I could possibly hope to alleviate the grief that I could see very clearly, but did not begin to understand.

You can always come to me and talk, she said. About anything.

Cate squeezed my arm. I thanked her.

She looked, then, down the passageway towards where he was sitting. I saw her face fall into lines of gentleness. It was love, I suppose, but I didn't think then that love was anything to take seriously. At that point in my life, I don't think that I had considered that anybody but myself had the capacity to feel things with any real integrity. The idea that Cate might have had her own inner life with all its vividness and self-doubt and vulnerability simply did not occur to me. And if it ever occurred to me that she might love him, I took far more seriously my own moments of jealousy and fury, more seriously the thirst that I felt for him, which I might have called love if I was forced to.

She was so easy to deceive. It would become, in time, so easy that I could imagine that she was a ready conspirator in all the

infidelities committed against her. She ended every text message she sent to me with *xx*.

Was it really possible she never knew? Did not know what had happened before, and did not know what was to come?

I stood up, left the living room, and walked past the bookcases and into the kitchen. I turned on the tap and emptied out the mug of wine into the sink. Through the grimy mosquito wire of the kitchen window I could see him in the passage, sitting on the milk crate and smoking my cigarettes. The others talked, but he did not. He was looking at me in the way you hope a man might one day look at you.

THE NEXT MORNING I spoke on the phone to a writer I'd been asked to interview for the literary magazine. I sat the digital recorder next to my phone on the eiderdown and I tried to summon all the focus and brightness of my academic self before dialling. But I needn't have worried. The writer took me seriously. He answered all my questions, even seemed to think my remarks were sometimes clever. At the end of the interview, when all my questions had been answered, the writer asked me if I had ever had anything published in the magazine I was representing.

No, I faltered. But I write. Or, I try to write. I finished my degree in November. I'm trying to write more seriously, is what I mean to say.

Well, he said, I think as soon as you unlearn everything they taught you at university, you'll be ready. I'm serious. As soon as you leave all that crap behind, you'll be fine. Don't go any further. Don't do a Master's or a PhD or whatever.

Oh, I said, I was thinking about applying for a PhD next year.

I don't know about that. I mean, it depends on what you want to be. Between you and me, there's a problem with their language, academics. You become too narrow in your language if you go down that path, you know?

Oh, um. I don't know. I studied English? I guess that's what I'd do the doctorate in.

Oh Christ! You need to go and hang out with some serious bogans for a while. If you did English at Sydney Uni, you need to go live on a housing estate for two months. Get some access to authentic voices.

Well, my part-time job is taking Triple Zero calls, I said, as though this might amount to the same thing.

Oh there's a story! There's a story. He paused, to consider the story. Yeah. Take a call, someone dies, and you stop on the way home at McDonald's drive-thru. That's the real stuff of life.

I liked this idea of the writer's; that I was in some way undercover in the real world, reporting from the front lines of my own experience. That I wasn't really an Emergency Services Answer Point Representative so much as I was temporarily playing the role of one. And wasn't that the point of the notebook? Wasn't that the idea with all the stories I read, the information I recorded? To pin it all down in syllables and sentence structure so that I could employ the experience for later use. But I was hesitant to consider my job with quite the degree of distance he was able to apply to it. Because when did temporary become permanent? The idea that I was gaining *experience* implied that I was different from everyone else who worked there. That I thought I was better than the job, above it. I spent all the time I could with the notebook beside me when I took calls, but the reality of my everyday life was the tripartite desk and the ringing of the phone, and at the end of it all, that was what it would say on my tax returns. I was no different from anyone else who worked there, and my experience was the same as theirs. I was just the one writing it down.

THE STAFFROOM of the call centre had walls made entirely of glass. The city wavered in its panes, pigeon-streaked and empty. From the Telcom-grey couches I could see the buses taking off down below on Elizabeth Street. It had just gone seven, and I was taking my break. I sat watching the streetlights switch on and slowly take possession of the city. The ABC news intro music began to play. In the staffroom, the television had sound.

Earlier that day cardinals had attended Mass in Rome before moving into the Sistine Chapel where they would commence voting for a new pope. Kim Jong-un had threatened to wipe out a neighbouring South Korean island in "a sea of fire". The New South Wales government had announced that it planned to lift the ban on fishing in all but one of the state's marine parks. And a committal trial had been held at the Magistrates' Court in Melbourne earlier that day. Evidence had been presented which had never before been shown to the public. A blue hoodie. A handbag found dumped in an alleyway. A SIM card found in possession of the man on trial. The man had pled not guilty to the charge of murder, but guilty to one count of rape.

When the woman went missing in Melbourne six months earlier, the story was everywhere. It was in all the papers, third or fourth in the seven o'clock news headlines, and then bumped up in the late edition to first. She smiled out from the photograph all the news organizations had seized upon. She was Irish, a beautiful, small-boned woman with a pink smile, a creamy face. Black hair.

I had first heard about the woman the day after she disappeared. Her face beamed out from the screen of my phone. The

Herald explained that she hadn't been seen since she left a bar on Sydney Road in Brunswick in the early hours of Saturday morning. I refreshed my phone every hour for more news of her. Eventually, it was all I could do. I didn't read. I didn't write. I didn't talk to anybody else.

Three days after she disappeared the police released CCTV footage taken from inside a bridal store on Sydney Road in Brunswick where the woman's last known movements had been captured. The first moments of the film were unremarkable, but then a figure in black tights and coat walked by the front window and you just knew it had to be her. Cars glided along the high edge of the frame. And then a man. There was a space between them. He was asking her something. He was, quite clearly, a stranger to her. Her heels were very high, and she walked in that way you're forced to when your feet are aching and all you want is to get home and feel something soft against your skin. At the end of the clip she turns and looks back. She looks back. But she follows him just the same.

It was around then that Clemmie began walking home with her keys wedged between her fingers. It'll fuck somebody up, she had told me. You just needed to aim correctly. Stab flesh. Hit bone.

At around ten p.m. on Friday, nearly a week after she had disappeared, a man led the police to the place where he had buried her. It was the hottest night of the month. The temperature had risen to 34°C in the middle of the day and it wouldn't go down. On the news they explained what had happened. She had been snatched off the street. Raped and murdered in an alleyway off Sydney Road. The man who'd done it had driven to the outskirts of Melbourne and buried her by the side of the road. He had done this sort of thing before, but this was the first time anybody had wound up dead. Brawny and ginger-haired, with faded tattoos, he had cried all through his police interrogation. He was

furious with himself. He was ashamed at being a "big sissy man". He said that he had done it because she had flipped him off. "That made me angry," he said. "Because I was actually trying to do a nice thing." He was a man who described himself as a Buddhist, who dug ditches for a living, and in his social media profile quoted the words of an aikido master: "Power of mind is infinite, while brawn is limited." He was a man who had told another woman—a woman he had raped but not killed—"See, look who's got the power" as he held her down.

The police exhumed her body at dawn. There were pictures on the websites of *The Telegraph, The Australian, The Age*. Early morning. Soft orange grass in the breaking light. Men with guns and shovels.

I watched and rewatched the footage of the woman in Brunswick taken outside the bridal shop. I always wondered why she looked back. Maybe she had wondered for a moment. Maybe it had felt like there was a world of possibility open to her on that street. Maybe, for the length of the fifteen-minute walk she had intended to take, she had longed for the darkness and the freedom of the shadows. Shadows where she thought she might pass unseen.

Arguably I had paid too much attention to the case. I could not un-remember many of the facts. I knew that after killing the woman in Brunswick the man had sat down in the laneway beside her and cried. I knew that before he had strangled her he had thrown her over the bonnet of a car and raped her where she stood. I knew that when he had been arrested last September he had, towards the end of the ten-hour interview, told the police: "They should have the death penalty for people like me. How many chances does a person need? They should never have let me out."

Once her body had been found the intensity leached out of the television stories and the newspaper reports and the social media posts. She had been found. People marched down Sydney Road. They left bouquets of flowers and notes of condolence. An arrest had been made. A prosecution was being prepared. Now that she had been found she had been transformed into a case, and people understood the narrative through-line of a case. But the onset of the case and the footage of the courtroom on television that evening did not cause me to think about her any less. The handbag. The footage from the bridal shop. A strand of hair struck by the sun for a moment on a back road outside the city limits, caught on a blade of grass. I thought about the woman in Brunswick all the time. Something about what had happened to her felt personal. From the staffroom of Triple Zero I leant forward as the ABC News focused on the man's face. As though if I could get close enough, I might be able to understand why he had done it. I was interested in the kind of man who hunts a girl, throws her down, weeps, leaves her body and walks away, returning to the world as ordinary a man as he had always been.

C OME OVER, he said, and so I did.
 Smoking a cigarette, I stood waiting for him out the front,
and when he opened the door he folded me up in his arms, Hey
you, so that I set my eyes, stubbed out the cigarette, and strode
ahead of him inside, so as not to let him know how nice it felt
to be folded up.

We settled out in the back passage with a view of the garden.
He told me about the play he was writing.

Are you happy with it?

No. I don't know. I'm afraid of failing.

You're too young to have failed properly.

Not that kind of failure. Not, like, failing to build a cathedral.
Failure like doing the wrong thing. Wronging other people.
Lying, cruelty, avarice. Those kinds of things. Small failures.
Moral imperfections.

I don't think you'll fail anyone by writing a play.

Maybe.

In the end, I don't think Lachlan ever made much of his
playwriting, although I hear that he is now a fairly well-respected
academic. He publishes his poems sometimes. I never read them.
But there have been no further plays. I do not know if that counts
as failure, although the way he personally defined failure was
always strange to me. He was so worried about trying to be good,
because, I suspect, he knew that he wasn't capable of ever really
being so. None of us are.

The blotting darkness in the courtyard absorbed the green
of the oleander. The ground was scattered with leaves that were
gradually decaying against the walls of the back passage. A herb
garden wilted by the fence.

You know, he said. The truth is, and it sounds arrogant. When I read *The Tree of Man* I thought, I can do this. I already write like Patrick White. And I can do *better* than him.

He emphasized his point with the orange tip of the cigarette he was smoking. I must have laughed at him. But what I remember most clearly now is that he brushed a finger against the bare skin of my arm as he spoke. As though to disguise a command with an entreaty. So I was not listening to him speak about *The Tree of Man*, or if I was I was only half listening, because in the dark of the garden under the banana tree I was remembering what it felt like to want to peel off the last layer of myself and surrender to him. To whatever he was asking for. I recognized that there was something trite and insipid about these feelings. Something wrong-headed, nonsensical, after all that had happened. But his voice still sounded like Home and swollen rivers and frozen glaciers to me. Nothing erased the fact that I felt, very sharply and so clearly that I lost track of what he was saying, that I wanted to do anything I could to stay with him.

You know it never would have worked, between you and me, he said. Last year. I'd have hurt you terribly.

I know. It hurt enough, what happened.

I'm sorry.

I ran my fingers through my hair and shook my head. What I remembered was the morning of the abortion. That I had wanted to stay, but I had left him there sleeping. I remembered that the bedroom ceiling had been high and lonely and my skin had turned to gooseflesh when I walked out of his bedroom and into the street. How he had not responded when I said that I was afraid.

Recently, when he was drunk, Lachlan had brought up that morning, nine months earlier. Not the abortion, but that he had

woken up and reached out for me and I was not there. He had expected to touch a warm body, but there was no body to be found. Just a note. He implied that my absence in his bed had wounded him. And this had both touched and angered me, so that I didn't know which emotion was the correct one to express, and so said nothing.

While he opened another bottle of bad red wine in the kitchen I walked into the space between kitchen and living room, filled entirely with bookcases. I could see in the corner of my vision that he was standing in the door frame, looking at me. I knelt down to examine the bottom shelves, and when I stood up straight he was behind me. He handed me a glass of red wine. This is the only wine glass we have, he said. He inched closer to me. I pointed to a thin, clean copy of a Knut Hamsun novel. This is nice, I said. You've read it?

A woman gave it to me a few years ago, he said. She said I would find it instructive. But I never read it.

I turned to him and smiled and found that his mouth was kissing-close to my throat.

My housemates and I combined our books, he said. Together we have all of literary theory. I began to laugh and he flushed a little, realizing how pompous he sounded. Well, there aren't many books at all here, are there? I said.

He rested a hand, very lightly, on the small of my back. Are you staying? Lachlan asked.

I don't know. I have to work at eight tomorrow morning. Hand me that bottle.

He handed me the bottle. Come on. Don't be absurd. Call in sick. Stay here. It's late.

OK?

He nodded. Go. Call. I'll pour you a drink.

I picked up my phone and passed the overstuffed armchair where he was sitting now, balancing a glass on his knee. I'll stay with you?

He looked up at me and nodded.

I walked into the kitchen, called the managerial office in Melbourne, and told them that my father was very ill and I would not be at work in the morning. It occurred to me, of course, as I made the phone call, that what I was about to do was ill-advised. We are meant to have learnt not to stick our hand in the fire once it has burnt us—this is a fundamental lesson of childhood. But the burn seemed worth it, or the fire seemed interesting, or both. Perhaps I was the kind of person, like a banksia tree, that needed an occasional catastrophe in order to break open my outer shell, spread my seeds and grow. At the bottom of a bottle of wine, the analogy seemed sound. I tried to conjure some idea of Cate, of how hurt she would be by the betrayal. But I didn't care. These were ideas, concepts, which flitted through my mind, but made no impact on what I had already decided I would do. That is the problem with desire: it adheres to no timeline, operates within no narrative arc, and we rarely want the things we are meant to want.

I told them my father was sick, I said as I climbed the staircase to Lachlan's bedroom. I don't know why I told them that.

I thought you didn't speak to your father?

No. Not really. But I might if he was about to die.

I put my bag down by his desk, slid my shoes off, and sat on his bed with my legs spread out. The breeze stirred the narrow leaves of the paperbark tree outside in the street. He sat down at his desk chair, took a swig from the bottle and passed it over to me. He exhaled, his breath catching. The flame from his lighter cast shadows on his face as he lit another cigarette. He stretched his legs out so that they almost touched mine.

And watched me.

The house had become very quiet. Only the sound of the rustling leaves and his breathing. I pushed my hand through my hair.

Don't do that, he said.

He wasn't looking at me so much as he was looking at the bookcase by the bed.

Don't do what?

You know well, what.

He rubbed his hand against his chin, and the gap between his bottom front teeth was hidden from my sight.

My hair is in your bed, I said. I could see the strands in the lamplight.

He put his head in his hands. What's wrong? I asked.

Nothing's wrong.

OK.

Jesus Christ. He stood up. Come on, he said, let's go to bed.

He turned off the light and in the dark I pulled off my skirt and shimmied beneath the doona. He slid in beside me, wearing only his underwear.

He propped himself on his elbow and looked down at me in the darkness, in which the forms of our bodies were resolving as our eyes adjusted to the night.

What are you looking at? I whispered.

Your hair.

I could not tell what he was feeling, but whatever it was his expression indicated that it was felt as extremely serious.

I can't tell, I said. Whether you're looking at the wall behind me, or my hair.

He smiled. You can pretty safely assume I'm looking at you and not the wall.

His hand was in my hair. He had a handful of it. There's so much of it. These are locks that I'm holding. Locks of hair. He did not let go, he continued to hold my hair in his hand.

Just look at you, he said.

A fumbling that seemed to rise and overflow. A comfort of hands and hair in the bedclothes. He spoke. I can't remember now what he said, only the sound. He spoke in that voice which seemed to promise that he could refreeze the ice pack and replenish the floodplains. And I wanted whatever I thought the promise was, wanted the form of him, wanted, just wanted, in staggering abundance.

Why do you always come to bed in tights? he said, reaching and pushing them down my hips.

Only with you, I said.

Do you sleep in tights when you're alone?

Of course not.

Take them off then.

Lachlan.

And the tights were off.

Are you OK?

His hands ran up my arms, my waist, my breasts. I love you, he said. I love you but I can't.

Don't say that. That's not the truth.

He said it again. And we did it anyway.

Are you leaving? he asked in the morning when I inched out of the bed.

I don't know, I said. You probably have work to do.

Later, sure. But, we could eat? Unless you don't like to eat with people who you've just.

I covered my eyes with my hand. He grinned. Come on, get dressed, he said.

We walked up to Erskineville Road. At the coffee shop on the corner we ordered and I sat on a stool, trying to keep my legs out of the way of other people, looking at the folded front

page of the *South Sydney Herald*. He sat beside me, and through my hair I could see him staring. What is it?

Do you have any brothers and sisters?

I began to laugh, and stood up to collect my latte from the counter. Hang on, he said. I have something coming with bacon in it. Are you sure you don't want anything to eat?

I'm happy with coffee.

The sun on the street outside struck blue and bright through the sparsely leaved plane trees. I sneezed, once, then twice, then three times. He watched me, an amused expression on his face which was unaccompanied by laughter. Are you done?

The sun makes me sneeze, I explained. When it's at an angle. Usually I have sunglasses, but not. Not now. I didn't think I'd need them last night when I.

We were walking together uphill, by the animal hospital and the ambling young mothers and the rippling pepper trees. He brushed his hand along my forearm.

I have to get a couple of things, if you don't have to rush off anywhere?

No, I mean. I can come.

You really sneeze in the sun?

Yes.

I've never heard of that.

Well, I do.

In the condiments aisle at the back of the supermarket we stood side by side staring at the different kinds of chilli sauce available. I turned to find him already looking at me. You all right? His face bent close to mine. And then all at once.

No no, he smirked after a moment. No kissing in the condiments aisle.

A T PEAK HOUR, when the call volume was at its highest, the television was switched to *A Current Affair*. All over the eastern seaboard people were leaving work, crashing their cars, and beginning to drink. I had only just begun my shift. It was the first chilly night of autumn, but there was no sign of it inside, beneath the central air conditioning vents. I was sitting on a tripartite desk with two men I rarely spoke to. They talked about football, mostly, and which sandwich they were going to buy from Subway during their break. They were the pair that Pat, on my first day, had labelled the dumbest fucks here. On the other side of the office beside the windows, I heard the same woman explaining that the city's water was polluted, and that's why she only drank bottled water. The water from the dam at Warragamba is full of cocaine and greyhound blood, she said.

Chicks are crazy, muttered one of the dumb fucks.

In the early years of the new Australian colony, one of the priests stranded down there at the edge of the island continent decided to carry out a survey of Sydney's women. Naturally, he included only European women, because according to him they were the only ones that counted. The priest drew up the "Female Register" and submitted it back Home to the British government. In the Female Register the priest found there were just two types of Australian women. The priest counted 395 wives, and 1,035 whores.

When I answered the phone the man on the line was yelling already. You hung the fuck up on me what the fuck do you think you're doing?

I explained that it had not been me he had just spoken to, and asked which service he required. He asked whether I was both stupid and a bitch. He suggested that the emergency services were incompetent. He had called for the ambulance before, he said, but now he wanted the police.

Fuck you pricks, he said, when I asked him what state and town his emergency was in. Macquarie Fields, he said when I repeated the question. I connected him through to the police. The line rang and rang. "Fuck you pricks" I wrote in the notebook.

The police will answer as soon as they can, I said.

What the fuck, he screamed. What the fuck.

The phone traffic was high. After nine unanswered rings, I said, I'm trying another line.

Every three repetitions of the dial tone I repeated, as directed, the police are still connecting please stay on the line. The presenter's hair on the silent television above looked like hard-boiled caramel. She nodded encouragingly at her co-host.

The man's angry yells became groans. What the fuck is taking so long? he asked. I assured him that the police would answer. The digital clock suspended from the ceiling flicked to 18:35 and Maeve logged off, waving goodbye to me as she exited the room. I waved back as I changed lines.

His breathing became hoarse. I can't fucking breathe, he whimpered. I can't fucking breathe. I asked if he would prefer to reconnect to an ambulance. But he didn't reply.

"I can't fucking breathe" I wrote in the notebook.

The police answered the phone then. But the man now didn't, or couldn't, respond. There was laboured breathing on the line, then the clattering of a phone falling out of a hand.

The caller asked for the police, I said, but he said he can't breathe and he hasn't responded since.

Did he say where he was? asked the police dispatcher.

Macquarie Fields.

No street address?

No.

Thanks, operator, I'll deal with it. Hello? Can you hear me?

I couldn't hear the man's breathing anymore when I hung up the phone.

While out in the middle of nowhere on his search for the inland sea, Oxley one morning instructed the accompanying botanist to dig some holes in a clearing. The men planted quince and peach and apricot seeds in the barren soil. They didn't expect that the trees would grow. After all, they had read their copies of Bacon and Locke. They were rational men. The quince and peach and apricot seeds were a gesture of hope. A hope rather than an expectation that the European trees would mark the passage of European men, "should these desolate plains be ever again visited by civilized man, of which, however, I think there is very little probability."

On the silent television a new segment began. A heavily fake-tanned woman was shown looking out a window, and then it cut to a scene of her gazing across the rows of cars in a Woolworth's parking lot. When she was interviewed under studio lighting her makeup appeared so thick it seemed to be smeared onto her face with a trowel. *A Current Affair* had been running a story for a week about this woman, who was alleging sexual assault by three Sydney football players. Or I thought that was what she was alleging. The television being silent, I was not sure of the specifics.

The men at the nearby phones were talking about the woman on the screen. They seemed to know all the details of the story. They were concerned about how her allegations would impact

upon the general morale of the team. The team stood for everything they wanted the country and themselves to be—strong, secure and mindless. I mean, she's probably lying, said the one with the thinning Thai hair transplant.

Australia's "first novelist" Marcus Clarke wrote once about those men like Oxley who had landed on the eastern shore and pushed off alone into the wilderness. He had imagined this figure of the ideal man, knowing that "he was lord of that wilderness, that in it he could live unmolested and secure, that he could find there a home and subsistence, with no aid but that of his own hands and his own brains." Men like Clarke believed that the effort of taming the natural world chiselled out "the whole man" from the poor marble of his birthright. Like women, the bush came wild or tamed, and they knew which one they preferred.

Why do you think she's lying? asked the thin one.

Well look at her, said the man with the hair transplant. They both looked up at the screen, at the woman with her eyeliner and leather boots silently explaining what had happened to her.

She's a fuckin' bitch. And she looks like that? She's asking for it.

The thin one sounded tentative. You really think stuff like that?

Yeah. Course.

"She's asking for it" I wrote in the notebook.

After the eruption of Mount Vesuvius destroyed the city of Pompeii, Christians at the time argued that it could be explained by the sacking of Jerusalem by Rome several years earlier. The sacking of Jerusalem had angered God. The destruction of a city filled top to bottom with Romans was, to Christian minds, divine punishment. It was nothing to get upset about, because

only sinners had died. The pure were pure by virtue of their being alive. It was a fantastically reassuring system of logic. God was good and catastrophe made sense. If you had been hurt, you must have been asking for it.

A CONVERSATION with Maeve:

Hey, are you working tomorrow? I know we said we'd get dumplings but New Shanghai is not going to happen this week. Maybe in the future when you're feeling nostalgic for Ashfield we can go, but I've got too much on this week.

No problem. And no, I'm not working until Sunday now. I switched some shifts around. I'm in bed. I need some time to try and calm down. I was so stressed out at work last night I was shaking and misdirecting calls.

Why so stressed?

I'm not sure. General malaise? Maybe everything. I'm trying to breathe.

Good idea. Also, try to use work as an opportunity to not think about things. I did it during uni. It was a lifesaver.

Yeah. You know the guy who gets the hair transplants? I saw him on his phone this morning, online shopping for knives. And not butter knives. Properly scary ones.

WOODEN STEPS LED down from the veranda and into my mother's garden. Along the side of the house the fernery grew dense and thick. The paving was all broken, the cracks striped with dirt and weeds. I trailed my hand along the bricks of the house as I walked. Moss grew so thick there, where the hose coiled out of the wall, that when I pressed down it felt sometimes like I was penetrating flesh. There was a scent of crushed insects and soil and decomposing blossoms. It felt very close, down in the thick of the garden with the din of crickets just starting as the light leaked out of the day. My mother stood halfway down the side of the house, directing the hose towards the tibouchina tree, her bare feet wet with the mud she was making.

This is pretty, I said, fingering the grevillea peeping out of the shadow of the tall grasses. She turned, and smiled. I'd hug you but I'd get you wet, she said.

That's all right.

It was comforting to simply be around her. I reached out and smoothed her hair into place, as she did with mine.

I'll go check on dinner.

I left her alone down there with the hose. She was smiling.

My mother liked to call her garden a jungle. She wanted it green and dense and impenetrable. This was curious to me, because she had expressed no interest in gardening when she was younger, or even when we lived in the house on the edge of the national park with my father. But that changed after the fires of '94, which had scorched the grass and trees of the garden without passing the property lines. She hadn't cared about that garden. She had done nothing about the scorched grass. But after we

moved into the house in Ashfield, my mother began working on her jungle with a terrifying affection. It had three big gum trees already well established, but not much else to speak of. In that first year alone, she planted bougainvillea vines, the tibouchina tree, bromeliads, *Monstera deliciosa*, birds of paradise and jasmine. After the burglary she had higher fences built along the side of the house that bordered the street. I was not allowed to leave the house and play outside under any circumstances, nor to play in the park across the street, and certainly not to walk unsupervised to the more exciting park three blocks down. Instead, my mother built me a swing in the back garden. She grew plants along the border of the fence. She did battle with the gum tree roots that rose up and unsettled the plumbing and the paving stones. And by these methods, she learnt to love the thing she had brought under her control.

But after a year or so the gum tree roots would grow back. They would unsettle the pipes and disturb the foundations of the house. The gum trees posed such a problem that she decided, in the end, to have them cut down. I recall my mother standing on the veranda on the afternoon that the men came with their chainsaws to cut down the trees. She smiled. As though she knew that, to keep herself feeling safe, the garden had to be defended. And now there were no gum trees in the garden, just plants and vines and ferns, and a fig tree which she could easily control.

When my mother finished hosing she wiped off her feet and came inside, moving back and forth between cupboard and worktop, assembling a dressing for a salad. On the veranda I set the table and set out a plate of foil-wrapped fish. Slices of lemon stuck to its scales. My mother thrust salad servers into my hands.

We stayed out on the veranda together for several hours, talking and drinking wine while the leftover fish leaked its juices

into the foil. My mother asked about my shift at the call centre earlier that day. I told her it was fine. She asked how I was coping with the work. She asked whether I thought it was helping with the writing. I tried to reassure her that it was, although writing had become increasingly difficult. But I didn't want to worry her, because my mother was already concerned about how I was coping with the calls. She didn't need to know the ways in which they affected everything else.

It's not the kind of job where you can sit around and reflect, I told her. It's not my place to take the calls personally. They aren't anything to do with me, I just put them through and make sure they get to the right place.

A look of doubt came across my mother's face. It was all there in her expression. The knowledge that a person can become lost in their life, how you might swim in the waters and reach for the lifebuoys but never be rescued, might drown out there in the dark ocean of your choices.

Before we moved to the house in Ashfield, my mother and I had lived with my father in a house that hugged the edges of Ku-ring-gai Chase National Park. We lived there together until the fires of '94. And then we left.

My mother and I had rarely discussed our leaving. The night she had woken me in the dark while he thumped on the door. The night she told me I had to be quiet, opened my bedroom window, and climbed down to the driveway outside, holding me in her arms. While he thumped and threatened to break the door down. You can't take her, he screamed. I won't let you take her. I'll kill you before I let you take her. I think she must have assumed I had been so young that year that I couldn't remember what had happened. But I did.

All my first memories were formed in that house on the edge

of the national park, in those days or maybe months when the fires were burning and my father's anger seemed to mount with the heat and the blood-red sun and the orange glow of the skies.

I recall one night perhaps two weeks before we left, listening from bed as the screaming carried on outside the boundaries of my closed bedroom door. I could not sleep amid so much screaming and the smell of smoke that issued through the mosquito netting. So that night I left bed and I walked downstairs.

I approached the sound of my father's voice, and through the crack between the rolling door and the door frame I could see him looming over my mother. I knew without a doubt that he was about to hit her. She was on the sofa, sobbing, her legs tight together as though she was trying to make her body smaller, and he was red and sweaty with the screaming he was doing. His arm was raised. He was bigger than her, and stronger. I rolled aside the door between the rooms and marched into the living room. I recall that I was clinging to a doll, barefoot, in my pyjamas. I stood between my parents and put my hands between them and said, Stop. I thought at the time that this was a terribly brave thing to do, and while I knew that the situation was serious, I did not appreciate how dangerous things had become.

But I understood something from the way my mother picked me up, the sound she made as she watched the little girl with curly hair stand between the two adults and put out her hands as though she could halt what was happening.

A howl.

She gathered me up in her arms and took me from the room, and I remember as she cried into my hair that I told her I was just trying to help. That night she slept with me in my small pink bed.

She was afraid of being alone with him. She slept with me not because she felt the need to protect me, but because I was warm and alive and some kind of comfort.

Even when we moved to the house in Ashfield she was building tall fences and looking out windows. She couldn't sleep deeply. She was waiting for him to appear at the door, to jump the fence, to smash through the glass of the back door. She had never ceased to be afraid of him.

From her chair on the veranda my mother twisted around and pointed the remote control for the stereo through the open back door. She turned the music up. The turning up of the music signalled that she was on the verge of becoming excessively and sentimentally drunk. We had, I assessed, drunk three bottles of wine between the two of us. She scrolled through to a song by INXS. A cockroach scuttled along the deck below her feet.

The INXS song played and she began to tell me the same anecdote she had told me so many times before: When I was six months pregnant with you I was driving to a party, and INXS was playing on the radio. I felt you begin to kick. But you were kicking in time to the music. You were dancing to INXS, right there in my stomach.

I know, Mum. I've heard.

I had told her I was thinking of going away, although I had not yet decided where I might go. I knew the idea that I might leave would make her sad. In fact she had said so.

I'm going to be all alone.

She held her glass of wine in both hands. Her teeth had turned purple. Have you spoken to your father about moving away?

We haven't spoken since Christmas. But no, though I don't imagine he'd object. It won't really affect him. Besides, it probably won't be for long.

No, I suppose not. But. You're not afraid? Of being some-where completely by yourself? What if something happened

to you? I worry, you know. You're self-destructive, and you're stubborn. I know you're clever, but you're reckless. You do things that at your age I would never have done.

This was what my mother had never understood. The things she never would have done—moving out of the city, dropping out of the university system and into paid-by-the-hour work, reckless sex and drinking—they were not things I did because I didn't know any better. I just didn't think there was any point in trying to shelter myself. If working on the phones had taught me anything, it was that emergency could not be avoided. Emergency would come for you no matter what you did.

Why did you ask about my father, I said. Have you spoken to him lately?

No, she said. A great sadness came over her, and a kind of weight settled across her shoulders.

What's wrong? I asked.

Nothing, she said. I'm drunk. Only that thinking about him, your father, it makes me so sad sometimes. I'm not sure I've ever loved anyone like I loved your father. I love my husband now, I do, but it's different. Sometimes I think that your father was the love of my life.

Really? After everything? Everything that he did.

The everything settled between us, solidly outlined, but unmentionable. The affairs, the amphetamines, the violence. The early-morning escape in the dark.

Yes, she said simply. And began to cry.

I have thought about that conversation with my mother often in the years since.

Throughout my childhood, I had longed for my mother to be able to present me with a self-contained narrative about what

had happened during that period of the fires in '94. I wanted her to explain with all the fervour of my child-self who still believed she could put up fences and grow the garden and make us safe. But of course, she could not.

CERTAIN PROMISES are made to us as children. Only in adulthood does it begin to dawn on us that many of those promises cannot be kept. The promise that the fairy godmother will rescue the protagonist, that the handsome prince will wake us with a kiss, that the wicked will be punished for the bad things they have done.

There are lower-level promises as well. For instance: that there exists a human-scale equivalent of "stationarity", which will keep the waters from ever rising too high and keep the fires from burning any more than is necessary. That rain will fall and the crops will grow and the tide will ebb and flow along an unchanging shore. That summer will come at the same time every year.

I was just young enough, that year, to still feel the sting of the betrayal that the promise could not be kept. I was becoming aware of the fact that the fires were vicious and the waters would not abate. That the thousand-year storms were just going to keep rolling in.

My mother could not give me a self-contained narrative, particularly not when she was weeping, particularly not when she was drunk. In a narrative there would be a clear ending. The scene would fade to black, the curtain would come down, the paragraph would break.

But our lives contain no line breaks. Our experiences are so frequently unbearable to us because real life is just sheer bloody continuity. The excruciating thing is not to have witnessed the person you love commit, upon your person or another's, an unforgivable act. The excruciating thing is that time carries on and you love them anyway.

I N THE MORNING stripes of light slanted through the gap
between the French door and floorboards in his bedroom.
The birds screeched in every tree on the street. I curled into the
crook of his arm, half sleeping. Hair pinned beneath his arms.
A stretch and twitch of stiff bones as my skin drew close to the
heat of him.

Morning, he whispered into my ear.

Hi, I said.

You sleep all right?

Yes.

He played with my nipple. I watched it harden, rise and swell.
His hand on my waist. That's an interesting thing you're doing
with your hips.

We turned to face one another, and with my leg around his
he stroked my face and pushed his thumb between my lips.
I went under the sheets. I used my mouth, but he pulled me
back up.

What's wrong? I asked.

I don't want to come.

We paused a moment. I looked at his face. The wanting.

Yes you do.

He nodded, or maybe I want to believe, now, that he nodded.
I went back down, he put his hands in my hair, he came, and
I swallowed him.

When I crawled up from under the sheet I found that the
orgasm had worked some kind of change. He began to think
again. I lay beside him, but I was all of a sudden aware of my
nakedness. I covered myself. His mind seemed to work over a
complex problem while he stared at the ceiling.

He got up out of bed and walked towards the veranda and opened the door to the outside world. A rush of eucalyptus, smog and light invaded the bedroom. The birds screeched.

Want some coffee?

I looked out at him through my hair. OK, I nodded. I sat up and began to peel back the covers.

No, don't worry. I'll go out to get it. I'll be back in a bit, he said. Don't leave the room.

He squeezed my foot and did not kiss me goodbye.

When he was gone I stepped out of the sheets and pulled my jumper on. I walked around the room, trying not to make the floorboards creak. I saw myself in his mirror. It was very big, propped by the wall next to the desk, so that he must have been able to see himself as he worked. My hair resembled nothing so much as a bird's nest. Fresh bruises dotted my legs, not from anything he had done, probably just from knocking against a chair leg. My skin seemed to bruise, these days, at the slightest pressure. In the mirror I examined my reflection and tried to comb out the knots with my fingers. I watched broken strands of hair fall to the carpet. The framed photograph of Patrick White glowered down at me from the wall, as though to suggest that he was not pleased to see me again.

I turned to the floor and found my underwear twisted up in my tights. I untangled the fabric and pulled them on. My bra was somewhere by the bookcase. Piles of books rose beside the shelves. Dirty laundry spilled out of the open wardrobe door. His belt on the floor. A wooden beat-up bust of Christ sat by the bedside table with a chipped nose, hands in prayer. It was a starving Byzantine Christ. I fingered the broken edges of its face.

I did not think he would like me to look at his desk, but he was not there to stop me. A leather jacket hung over the back of the chair. Beneath the desk, a tangle of wires and unworn running

shoes, old boots, a plastic spoon. There were sticky spaces on the surface where sugary drinks had been left to sweat too long. A laptop with a broken charger was password protected. Two notebooks lay open. The pages were full of notes to self: "The problem with the essay can often become its subject." "I can't write as well as I'd like." A volume of Gore Vidal open to an essay on Italo Calvino, Russian fairy tales, *Demons* by Dostoevsky, dog-eared, a copy of *Elizabeth Costello* splayed, pages down, on top of other books. The spines were bent and creased. I ran my finger down the volume of fairy tales, as though by touching it I might be able to uncrease what had already been broken. Beside the Dostoevsky a copy of Saint Augustine's *Confessions*. Somebody had written on the first page, and I lifted the cover to read the inscription, written in thick black pen. *Cate, Katoomba, February, 2011.* I turned and moved away from the desk and the books, back to the bed where my hair was tangled in the bed sheets. There was nothing in that room with my name on it. Nothing to which I could stake a claim.

I lay in his bed for another half hour before he came back, with coffee. He handed it to me and stood by the bed, looking down. I reached out my hand and held on to his thigh. I looked up. His gaze would have been severe were it not so soothing. I pulled his leg towards me. He sank down to my level.

A bell jar of calm and order lowered down over the two of us in the bed. Inside the jar there was purpose, reason, a nature that adhered to the predictable order of things. We were safe.

Everything is going to be OK, he said, and while we were there in his bed there was no part of me that doubted him.

P AT LIKED TO CONCLUDE arguments with the same phrase—
You've made your bed, now lie in it. She liked to argue
about politics and the law, and she was often the winner of
the argument, although I do not believe in the time we worked
together I ever saw her change someone's mind. People's minds
don't bear changing.

There was a map of Australia in the call centre, pinned to a pylon
in the middle of the room. I suppose somebody once must have
thought it would be helpful for us to visualize the continent while
we were on the phones. The map listed the cities, and even big
towns. But knowledge of cities and big towns was never much
use. Because what the map didn't account for was that the most
important places were the small ones we had never heard of
before. Middle of nowhere. The great big empty. Back of Bourke.
The Never-Never. Whatever the fuck you wanted to call it.

The small, tricky towns produced stress. The stress of hear-
ing somebody scream for the police on a bad line, not knowing
what they were saying, and asking as they screamed if they
might be able to spell it. Wherever they were out there, wher-
ever they were having their emergencies. People died this way,
I told Lachlan, and Clemmie, but never my mother. In those
precious seconds when I didn't know and asked the caller to
spell the name of the town and they screamed and sometimes
ceased responding. Somebody must have died while I asked if
they could spell it.

One night on the television a segment detailed the risk to coastal
properties along the Northern Beaches. Homeowners were

having problems with their insurance companies. Their premiums were too high, because their houses faced right onto the beach. The insurance companies countered that the houses were at increased risk of inundation due to rising sea levels. The homeowners seemed to respond with something along the lines of "get fucked". Hard to tell. No sound on the televisions. The journalist cut to a map of the continent. It showed the country as it is now, and then the way it would look once the ocean got high. And indeed, the properties would be long gone, sunk below the surface, algae growing on the skirting boards, sharks butting up against the windowpanes. What do they expect? said Pat, nodding up at the screen. It's not like the insurance companies can stop rising sea levels. We've made our beds, now we're all going to have to lie in them.

I discovered sometime around then an uncommon map of Australia. The map was published to great interest in the 1820s, when the interior of the continent was largely uncharted.

The map had been commissioned by a man named Maslen, a retired employee of the British East India Company. He had never visited Australia. But he believed in Oxley's vision of the inland sea, because, like me, he had read the journals, and had a keen belief in the promise of Empire making its way. The landscape might have been back to front and the seasons all different, but the inland sea allowed everyone to believe that the prisonscape they had established in the Antipodes might really be a kind of pristine Eden, which God had set down on the earth as a gift to the British Empire.

Maslen's map shows a string of wide river systems penetrating the continent from the north-west, descending downwards to a wide-open sea in the middle of the country. All rivers flow to meet it. The northern part of the map is marked Australindia.

The southern part of the continent, Anglicania. The inland sea, Delta Australia.

Maslen commissioned the map because he was as sure of the logic of the inland sea as though it had already been navigated. He wrote to the colonial authorities in Sydney, enclosing a copy of the map, and proposed that the government should fund another inland expedition with his guidance. He suggested equipping men with camels and elephants and guns. These soldiers would cross from one side of Australia to the other, establishing small townships along the way, until the entire continent and her interior ocean was known and navigated in its entirety.

It made *sense* that there would be an inland sea. It adhered to fundamental theories of balance. Men like Oxley and Maslen assumed that the land was proportional. When it was at last understood that there was no Eden, no inland sea, that westward the course of Empire would never make its way, and that the island continent did not align with any prevailing theory of reason, then it was felt, if not made a point of law, that the land was just as wild as the kind of woman who's asking for it.

M Y MOTHER HAD MET Lachlan once, the day we gradu-
ated. She took a photograph of the two of us, standing
together beneath the jacaranda in the university quad. The
attrition of light as it pushed against sandstone, not violent, but
persistently gold. The native, neo-Gothic monsters that bore
down above us as we shifted awkwardly beside one another. In
the photograph we are smiling. Close, but not touching. Has it
occurred to you, she asked me later, that he resembles your father?

"DARLING DON'T YOU go and cut your hair," the radio played, again and again, between news updates during the week of the fires in '94, the month that my mother took me and left.

My mother and I listened to the radio, driving home from the city through the national park to the house we all lived in together, though for only a few weeks more. There was a blood-red sun hanging over the road that day. Ash clotted the air. We came to a traffic jam while the smoke plumed in the distance and the wind swept through the bush. "But I don't care, I care, I really don't care," spoke the radio. Firemen in their fluorescent suits walked along the sides of the road through the perilously yellow grass.

A rattling of gum nuts punctured the song as the wind picked up and they flew at the roof of the car.

One of the firemen in his bright yellow jacket approached my mother's window and she rolled down the glass. He informed her that the fire had jumped containment lines and was burning out of control. They were closing the roads. Ash clung to the sweat of his brow, and I remember that it didn't seem to bother him. My mother wished the fireman good luck, and we turned back, with the rest of the traffic. We drove to my grandparents' house. I recalled the song from the radio when I stood on their driveway, looking out towards the north and west. The fire burned on the edges of the city and the red sun sank into the ash and cloud. I could smell the smoke in my just-cut hair.

That evening I sat on the gold filigree carpet of my grandparents' living room with the air conditioner on full blast, watching the over-saturated television set they had bought in the late '60s. On the ABC news I saw the fires burn in the bushland behind

the house where my father was. The manicured grass of all the gardens on the street was crisp, and blackening. I had looked for my father in the footage of the firefighters and the flames. I had naturally supposed that the fire had something to do with him.

My grandfather had sat behind me on the sofa while the ABC broadcast the inferno, a cold bottle of Crown Lager resting on the tiny table he reserved for that purpose. The incompetence of the fire service, for fuck's sake, he had yelled. No back burning, they don't know how to do the job, and now look where it's got the pack of bastards.

I did not ask him whether my father would be safe. He turned the television off. My grandfather went to the spare room, where my grandparents kept the films they had taped from television onto carefully labelled and alphabetized VHS tapes. My grandfather chose *Brief Encounter*, and that night we watched it together instead of the bushfires.

In the end my father hadn't even been at the house. He was safe from the fire. He was staying elsewhere, with a woman, in Bondi, I think, and shortly after the fires we would sell that house. My mother took me out of the suburbs and back to the city, while my father moved to Melbourne.

I still dream about that fire, sometimes. I still smell the smoke in my hair. In these dreams I find myself looking down the same stretch of closed-off road in Ku-ring-gai Chase National Park where my mother and I had been stopped by the RFS. In the dream, the flames tower around me. I never feel the heat in the dream, only a sense of animal terror, that my father is somewhere beyond the flames, that he cannot get to me, does not know where I am, and no one will be coming to save me from the fire.

O NE EVENING, at one in the morning, I returned home from the call centre and I was too tired to read. I poured wine into a glass, set my laptop on the bed, and found a full-length version of *Brief Encounter* on YouTube, which was watchable enough, although grainy. I had not watched the film since the VHS copy at my grandparents' house, which I watched often after my grandfather first showed it to me during the fires, on rainy evenings when I was sent to stay with them. I remember the film on the tape being split up by ads for bananas and toothpaste in the shoulder-padded, yellow-green lighting of the 1980s. My grandparents taped many films onto VHS tapes, but it never occurred to them that they could pause the recording during the ads.

I liked the film because it was so cautious, so small. Every scene occurred in a railway station, a drawing room, a cinema, a tearoom, as though all of England were nothing more than cramped spaces where middle-class lovers could gaze at one another in anguish. It was the sort of film it seemed strange to love now, because it was concerned with such small things, because it was so melodramatic, because it was so English. And they said the kinds of ridiculous things the English used to really believe, and perhaps still do. "You know," intoned Celia Johnson, "I believe we should all behave differently if we lived in a warm, sunny climate all the time. We shouldn't be so withdrawn, and shy, and difficult." Which was nonsense, I realized now. Misery thrives on sunshine.

Who *were* these people, I wondered, whiling away the Second World War with their shopping and missed trains and affairs?

But there was something so soothing about the film's small-ness. Its predictability. The affair would always end, the train

would always leave, but Celia Johnson never would find it within herself to throw herself onto the tracks.

The comfort of the film was mixed up with the ads for bananas and toothpaste that haunted my memory of first watching it, ads which I found myself anticipating as scenes faded out every fifteen minutes. The memory of the advertisements created lacunae in the film, and in my head the Australia of the 1980s — closer, but just as foreign — muddled itself with England of the 1940s, a soup of homesickness for times I'd never known. As if a time were a place you could return to. As if all those rituals my family had brought from England two hundred years ago, all those habits and rituals we fell into at Christmas, on birthdays, in times of crisis, could make sense of anything. And after all, the feeling had nothing to do with England as it was now—in London, years earlier, I had expected to find something to love, but all I found were grey days, and bad coffee, and a man who crossed the atrium at Shoreditch High Street overground station with no other purpose but to stamp his foot down on a child's untended balloon. Nothing was as promised.

From the standing desk in the corner, Maeve told me and whoever cared to listen that she had been reading accounts from people online who had eaten another person. Not cannibals as such. Just people who had found themselves in situations where they had, by necessity, eaten somebody. They said we taste like pork, but gamier, she said. There was one man, actually, from England, who'd had his hip replaced. So he took the old hip home, carved off the meat and cooked it in a sauce. Served it with pasta and a glass of wine. Emergency police, fire or ambulance?

All our conversations happened like this, broken up and punctuated by the sudden calm tones we were forced to adopt every time we recited the script.

How could he do that? asked Pat. I couldn't even take my wisdom teeth with me when I had them out. Once they remove something doctors won't give it back to you. It's considered medical waste.

Well, that's what he said. Maybe the laws are less restrictive in England.

Nothing is less restrictive in England, I said.

When I was eighteen, I had gone to England. I had thought perhaps that London was the place for me. But when I got there I found that it felt more like a mausoleum than a place I could envision my future. One evening I had gone to see a show in Shoreditch, alone. I spent the evening bumping against strangers who looked at me coldly, drinking too-sweet cider, sinking into the music which, anyway, was boring. After the show, I had walked up and down, through Shoreditch and the East End, as though

I were looking for the friends I hadn't met yet. But the friends failed to materialize in Shoreditch, or anywhere in England.

Another conversation with Maeve that morning:

Do you understand how incredibly fucking stupid it is to be sleeping with him again? Emergency police, fire or ambulance? Connecting police for Newcastle, New South Wales.

I know.

I mean, I don't know what you want me to say exactly. Because I think it's something that you sound like you're enjoying despite all the protestations and admissions of guilt. I think it's something that once you leave Sydney and get some distance from the whole thing you will be disgusted with yourself for. This is not something that a good person would do. And I think that all we can ever strive to be is a good person. I don't understand why you're doing it. I don't understand why Lachlan is doing it. There is nothing good that can come from it. You are both using each other. And this secrecy is just another component of the game. Cate will find out. You know she will. This is cruelty. I don't know whether you just want me to say it, but you know it's all true.

Emergency police, fire or ambulance? Emergency police, fire or ambulance? No response.

The frustrating thing from Maeve's perspective was that interventions by one's friends on behalf of morality, or goodness, or our well-being, matter so very little. I know now as I knew then that it was incredibly fucking stupid to be sleeping with him again. And I know now that our friends have little sympathy when we stick our hand in the fire again, when they've nursed us through the burns the first time around. Because why?

It is never easy to say, *because I want it*, and have that be enough.

I could have explained that I knew it wouldn't last, indeed,

I didn't expect it to. I didn't expect that it would end well, or that we wouldn't hurt one another. It was simply that I didn't care. I wanted, in the three-second pop-ups and hot-takes of attention I received, the sound of his voice and the infinitely reassuring way in which it warmed and rippled through me because in those moments it felt like the fragments were at last hung on a storyline, and that was what I wanted.

"You know, I believe we should all behave differently if we lived in a warm, sunny climate all the time. We shouldn't be so withdrawn, and shy, and difficult."

Celia Johnson was wrong. I knew it even when I was a child. Because I was from a place that was both relentlessly sunny, and difficult. A place where the weather got so warm it sometimes killed us.

There it is. Take it. So said William Mulholland to the assembled crowds in the San Fernando Valley the day he brought water to Los Angeles. It was a declaration full of longing and recklessness, made by a man who had followed through on his promise to bring rain to a dried out place, and who would spend his old age in mourning for the hundreds drowned in his single-minded mission to flood the desert. But wasn't his hubris infinitely reasonable? I understood the need to control water. I understood putting your faith in its ebb and flow and the devastation you might feel when it didn't work out as you'd hoped.

Los Angeles too was a warm, sunny place.

I booked my plane ticket this morning, I said to Maeve between calls.
 Really? Where to?
 America.

That's what you decided? Where in America?

California.

I was so sure you'd go to Europe. Why California?

Because it has nothing to do with me and I have nothing to do with it.

When are you leaving?

In November, three days after my birthday.

OK. But, really, America? California? Are you sure? That doesn't seem like you.

During my break that morning, two men standing on the corner of Castlereagh Street wore Guy Fawkes masks and grey hoodies and offered to explain to me how I could save my life by rising up against the church of Scientology. The headquarters sat across the road. They pointed to the large square windows from beneath the eaves where they sheltered from the wind. The masked men explained that the E-meters and the auditing and the Clears were brainwashing the vulnerable. It was a moneymaking scheme, where true believers scrubbed floors and surrendered their will because they believed in the promise of salvation.

They're all in league, one said.

Are you chill? asked the other.

Sure, I said.

I told them that I needed to go inside because my break was up. Have a lovely day, one called after me. He looked so cold, in his mask, while the wind whipped the winter up along Elizabeth Street from the harbour.

An hour later, as I walked through the glass doors and headed into the park for my longer lunch break, I saw that the men had abandoned their posts. They were standing in line for sandwiches in the Subway beside the headquarters. They still wore their masks.

I LEFT THE OFFICE late at night. The walk along Elizabeth Street was wet, but I didn't mind. The rain had poured down all day and now drizzled, as though it too were tired and needed to rest before the inundation continued. Lights glowed gold and red in the indigo sky like a promise just before it's broken. In the distance, behind the skyline, were the suburbs with their salmon bricks and paint blisters on woodwork and Colourbond fences kept in place by grids of buffalo grass. And beyond even that, the plains and the desert. I could feel it. A casual sort of violence seemed to vibrate beneath the highways, the warehouses, the gasworks and the high-rises.

I had not been home more than half an hour when I began to hear it. Outside on the street a loud sound. A crack.

And then another.

With every crack the darkness of the bedroom was flooded with light. Blue and bright and sickly. I stood at the window and looked out at the mechanic's and the paperbark tree and Elizabeth Street slicked wet by the rain. The sky's heart torn wide open. Blue light splintered the room. I could see, out there above the fig and the mulberry trees, the flash of light, and then the smoke.

The power line was on fire. The flame wasn't getting far with the rain, but I could see it directly in front of me through the window, the smoking electricity wires shaking in the wind. I tried the lights in my room and the power was dead. I noted that the smoking power line was connected directly to the black wires that terminated on the bricks by the bedroom windows.

My housemate Paul was still at work, and Joe was with his girlfriend. I was the only one home. I pulled a cardigan over the

lace petticoat I slept in and walked downstairs in the dark with my phone in my hand. I opened the front door and the iron security gate. The power line was still on fire. The flame licked the darkness. I dialled ooo.

I will do this properly, I thought. I knew the protocol. I wondered if I would recognize the voice that answered the phone. And would I say something? I had never been on this side of the line before. But I wasn't sure whose voice it was when the emergency services answered. I need the fire brigade for Redfern, New South Wales, I said. And was connected. I was the very model of a calm caller. The rain slanted in below the awning. My toes were wet, pale and then suddenly blue in the flash of electricity. The phone rang twice before they answered. I explained the problem to the fire brigade. They asked for my address, and told me to wait for them. They would be there soon. Happens sometimes when there's heavy rain, said the man on the phone. The water gets in and the lines short-circuit.

I stood under the awning, leaning against the arm of the couch that we never used, which sat beside the front door. The smoke and electricity were oddly pretty in the rain when seen through the canopy of slick, wet leaves, in the dark.

Whaddya think of that, said a voice. From beneath the grape-vines of the house next door the old Greek man emerged in his dressing gown. His wife, I supposed, was inside. I so rarely saw him, unless he was watering the tomato plants.

I called the fire brigade, they're coming, I said.

Well, I called the police about fifteen minutes ago. They haven't showed up yet.

I did not ask him why he had called the police. It seemed a patently ridiculous thing to do. When there's smoke, wouldn't you think of fire?

140

Well, they should be here soon, I said. I looked down at my phone.

He continued to stand there in the dark. The power line cracked and the rain came down. I could feel the old man looking at me. Now that he was there it was hard to be aware of anything else. He was big. His bigness the first and second thing you noticed about him. The third, his hair, the way the stubble grew grey and thatch-like across his chin and neck, out of his nose and ears, into his chest and down into the V of his dressing gown because he was not wearing any clothes beneath it. He watched me. I pulled the cardigan over my breasts, crossed my legs more tightly. He had wide hands and in the flashes of electricity his face shone. Ruddy, years of drink visible on the surface, the broken veins spread across his cheeks.

I'll just sit down here and wait with you, said the man. He took three steps from beneath his grapevine and came to sit beside me, where I leant on the arm of the couch. The grey chest hair overspilled the V of his tattered dressing gown, gaped wider. I felt his arm brush against my thigh. The electricity cracked blue again and the flame burning along the power line began to spread. I no longer felt like the model of a calm caller. I was all of a sudden caved-in. Tremendously alert, but vacant. Frantically empty. I didn't move, not at all.

I could hear the sirens approaching.

Your hair is very pretty, said the man. What's your name?

TREMOR

T HE FIRST PAPER on "Australian Matters" presented to the Geological Society of London was given in 1820 by the Reverend William Buckland. The paper included some observations on a series of rocks collected by John Oxley during his 1817 journey along the Lachlan River, and sent on to London upon Oxley's return to Sydney. It was unclear where, precisely, Oxley had obtained the samples, only that the land in question lay west of the Blue Mountains. Buckland, in his paper, described "A strong analogy between the coal formation of the Hunter's River and River Hawkesbury in New South Wales and that of England, which well deserves to be accurately investigated". This would prove to be a confusing analogy. New South Wales is not England, and Hunter coal is not English coal, but it would not stop anyone from reaching a hand into the navel of the earth and squeezing at any promising flesh they could find.

It might have made things easier on the men of the Geological Society if New South Wales were identical to England and its coal just as extractable. But they were soft men in shabby trousers more comfortable scrabbling on the beaches of the Dover coast for fossils, hoping like hell to stumble upon the jawbone of a dinosaur. The Antipodes were interesting only so far as they provoked moments of curious conversation in the Freemasons' Tavern at Covent Garden of an evening.

Shortly after Buckland delivered the first Australian paper to the well-read rock enthusiasts of London, the Geological Society came to be presided over by Charles Lyell, a mentor to the younger Darwin. Lyell instilled in the society one of the greatest tenets of Victorian science—the principle of "uniformitarianism". This was a principle in which it was supposed that the

earth changed at precisely the same rate and in the same ways as it had done in the past. The earth was Orderly and Consistent and could be mastered by Men.

But this orderly view of natural history put Lyell in philosophical conflict with the views of French geologists, who had recently proposed the concept of "catastrophism". Catastrophists saw the earth as formed by occasional violent cataclysms—floods, fires, earthquakes, heat. Lyell rejected all theories of catastrophism. Geological catastrophism was not far, in his mind, from the insult of the Jacobins across the Channel. Revolutionary hogwash. The theory struck him as pre-rationalist, and essentially un-English.

While Lyell was waging an ideological war in the form of rocks, his protégé Charles Darwin had set sail around the world on the *Beagle*. In the 1830s, the *Beagle* reached the north-west coast of Australia, one of the most catastrophic places on the globe—fire-prone, flood-prone, hot. The *Beagle* progressed fifty miles up the Victoria River, a river cherished today as one of the country's last remaining "wild" rivers according to the Department of Environment and Energy. After a few miles of red rocks and water and avian shrieks, the principal surveyor on Darwin's ship sent word back to England. Darwin and his men believed that this river of the north was the vein that might bleed into a central inland sea somewhere out there in the middle of the island continent.

They all believed. Believed in the warm, wet centre opening its legs out there in the heart of the dead, dry country. They could almost taste it, almost see it, the promise just beyond the horizon, sloganeering their hopes like a black swan at dusk.

Word of Darwin's theory reached Charles Sturt, who was then living in the city of Adelaide. From his home, Sturt had taken to watching the flight path of waterbirds. He saw the birds fly west from Sydney, and he saw them fly north from Adelaide. He

had developed a theory. He took a pen to a map of the known continent, and he joined together the lines of migration of the waterbirds, and found a point of convergence, a degree or so north of the Tropic of Capricorn.

When Oxley had returned from his journey down the Lachlan River and announced, "I feel confident we were in the immediate vicinity of an inland sea," Sturt was the first to drink my great-great-great-great-grandfather's Kool-Aid. Darwin jigsaw-puzzled with Sturt's lines of migration, with Oxley's journey west, with all those hunches and hopes that the land could be apprehended and subjugated to the will of men.

And so Sturt proposed an expedition into the interior. Twenty-seven years after Oxley's journey, Sturt, filled with conviction, led an expedition into the desert along with a twenty-five-foot whaleboat and two ex-sailors to man it. The wastes got barren and the rivers petered out into salt plains, but Sturt was ever hopeful. Space was made for conquering. The desert had to be other than empty. The river must flow backwards for a reason.

And so his men died. Thirst overwhelmed them. They developed scurvy. Their bodies' connective tissue disintegrated. Old wounds reopened. But Sturt smiled out of a face reddened by dust. He held faith with the questionable symbolism of birds. He believed he heard swans.

IN THE WINTER I was placed on morning shifts. Each day I woke up at four in the morning to be ready to take calls at five. The dawn was still a distant dream as I walked through the tall glass doors, swiped through at the security gates and took the lift up.

Mornings were slow, and I had found that I had come to like them. The staff were older in the mornings. They were the kind of women who'd make vanilla slice if there were a birthday, who brought in plates of cheese cubes and cabanossi, and referred to me as "love" because they couldn't remember my name. The women's voices filled the thin morning light with chatter of arthritis, the council and their wayward children. That morning the preoccupying outrage was the next-door neighbour's gum tree hanging too far over a shared fence.

It's a bloody accident waiting to happen.

Oh, yairs.

My word.

Emergency, police, fire or ambulance.

The night before, in my bedroom, I had watched the rain fall against the glass in thick, translucent veils. Buses heaved in the street below. I had missed a deadline for an essay I had pitched, but when I sat up in bed intending to write, I found I was unable. I instead lay in bed and listened to the fireplace. My body felt like it had all the consistency of water. I had been to a doctor on Glebe Point Road and she had run reams of tests on me. I was anaemic. The tests showed that I had an abnormal liver enzyme count. I had been told to stop drinking and to rebuild my iron levels. I also had chlamydia, and was prescribed antibiotics.

Do you know how you might have got it?

No.

Have you had unprotected sex lately?

With every single person I've ever slept with.

Don't do that, the doctor said. Anyway, the antibiotics should clear it right up.

The doctor advised that I consider my options, and offered to write a prescription for birth control, but I had demurred.

No hormones, I said. I am afraid they'll make me depressed.

At that, the doctor had shaken her head.

A flurry of calls came in the mornings as people began to wake up on the east coast. There were car accidents, angry motorists and loved ones who had taken ill during the night. Then a lull set in, between nine-thirty and eleven, when calls were infrequent. The television personalities began to move with a sedated languor, their smiles widened, and the segments on Tupperware, juicers and control-top underpants began. That's about the time that the old women would begin to call.

The calls tended to arrive in concert with postmen, midday marketers and door-to-door prophets. The old women would place calls to the emergency services, not knowing precisely what they wanted, but knowing they wanted something. Their voices simpered and quivered as they must have done in times of vulnerability since little-girlhood. The old women invariably believed that the voice they heard when I spoke was one of a police officer. They only grew more confused when I tried to explain that I was not. All the old women told a version of the same story. There's somebody knocking at the door, and, oh dear, I'm a woman all alone in the house and I'm terribly frightened. I'm all alone. Won't somebody please come and help me. Somebody's at the door and I'm frightened.

I put the calls through to the police.

All the while I connected them through, I wanted to tell them to open the fucking door. To talk to the postman, the Jehovah's Witness, the phone company. I wanted to tell them that they didn't need protection, and surely facing the man at the door, whether he was selling phones or brandishing a butcher's knife, was better than this helplessness and terror and the unwavering belief in these other knifeless men at the end of the phone who might care for them.

But in the moments between calls I would reason with myself. It is natural to be afraid of the man at the door, I wrote in the notebook. That's how humans evolved, after all. When a twig rustled in the leaves, it was the anxious ones who survived because they ran away regardless of whether the rustle had been caused by the breeze or a bear. You got on better if you ran away. And so we went on, evolved, creating stories to explain away the inexplicable. We said Vulcan was angry and that was why the volcano rumbled. We said that the swan was a portent of nearby water. We said that God punished the sinners and saved the virtuous. To acknowledge that terrible things happen and people are killed and tragedy befalls the good for no reason at all would defy all our expectations of narrative. So why not call the police on the Jehovah's Witness at the door, if it worked to stave off the terror that one day the man with the knife really might arrive, might not even knock on the door, and in the end it would signify nothing?

I sat looking through the office windows over the park. I watched the rain snap the City of Sydney flags, and the patent-leather leaves of the park rustle in the wind. On the television the ads were all for kitchenware and weight-loss supplements. I listened to the hum of the air conditioner and counted down the minutes on the overhead clock until my second break. Phones ringing.

Emergency police, fire or ambulance.

Um. Ok, so, I'm not sure. Um. Maybe you could help me?

Do you require the police, the fire or the ambulance?

Um, well. So. The thing is. I got a new dog. And the old dog was really excited to have a friend. A new friend. And um. Yeah. The dogs had sex with each other. But not. Yeah. One of them is pretty little. So. They're, um, stuck inside one another. So I don't know who can help me with that?

What state and town is the emergency in?

Dundas Valley. New South Wales.

Connecting to the police for Dundas Valley, New South Wales.

In the notebook I kept beside me I wrote down "pretty little".

T HE POOL in Prince Alfred Park was newly renovated, and because it had run millions of dollars over budget and been finished years late, the council was allowing free entry to local residents up until November. In the late afternoon, the benches surrounding the pool were half-full. It was winter, sure, but unseasonably warm. The deck chairs underneath the old trees attracted the kinds of women so beautiful that each one, separately, might cause you to lose your reason. Bronzed men performed push-ups in the grass by the fences.

I had taken to coming to the swimming pool every day, even when the weather was cold. I would lie on the benches with a jumper thrown over my swimming costume, reading or writing, but always in view of the water. I found the water infinitely soothing, and in those months it became the only thing that could calm me down.

I had always wanted a swimming pool as a child, but I was raised in drought conditions. Every year of my childhood the drought got worse, every year more crops failed, the reservoirs fell and television news was full of images of cattle ribs bleached white on the plains. When the state government instituted water restrictions, I learnt to take short showers, my mother watered the garden only after dark, and we did away with sprinklers and the hosing of driveways. But each weekend we drove to the ocean and I swam and the waves took me, rolled me under, and I emerged back onto the surface with a mouthful of salt.

It was infinitely clear to me even then that I lived in a country afflicted by a paradox. We were a people surrounded by water, living on one of the most arid continents in the world, a place

rapidly running out of potable water, with no hope of any inland sea to hang our hopes on anymore. The rain could not be coaxed from the sky, the dams could not be raised, empty ghost rivers like the Lachlan would never run steady again. And so I longed for rooms of steam, for baths, for the cool blue miracle of a swimming pool in which the water could be contained as though it were safe in the cup of your hand. When I came to the swimming pool now, I gazed at the water more than I read the book I brought with me. It was infinitely soothing, and looking at the swimming pool I could forget the emergencies, my confused plans and all the men in leather jackets or thongs or tattered dressing gowns who laid their hands on my body whether I wanted them to or not.

The changing rooms of Prince Alfred Park Pool had been built by the children's play area. Their shrieking echoed off the wet concrete floor of the locker room in which I was standing naked. In front of the mirror in the changing rooms I examined my body for marks.

I made an inventory.

There were, first, the bite marks on my neck. There were scratches that stretched down my back. Bruises in browns and pinks and purples. The bruises were patterned along my arms and legs as though on purpose. Sometimes I could remember their provenance. The corner of a desk had left its imprint on my hip. A stumble on the stairs had marked my calf with a long dark stripe. On my thigh there were five circular bruises, corresponding precisely to the largish fingers of a man's hand. The rest of the bruises were as indecipherable to me as a lover's thoughts.

A middle-aged woman eyed me from the other side of the changing rooms, then turned her eyes to the ground, fastening her

sweat-stained bra behind her back. I did not know how to read her face. Did she think I had been beaten? Was she sorry for me?

The bruises were from sex, and also a product of my recklessness. I was careless with my body when I was drinking and blacked out. I had blacked out in my bedroom the night before, and again, a week earlier, trying to feel comfortable, chill out or anyway hang loose with people from the call centre at a bar on Castlereagh Street. I couldn't remember what I had done, but in the morning my flesh bore the marks of the night.

The middle-aged woman slipped on her blouse and her black dress trousers and left, without saying anything or giving me another glance.

Once the woman was gone I could examine myself more closely. Staring at myself in the mirror, it occurred to me that my body might look a lot different by now. A kind of ghost life ran parallel with my own. One year. It had been a year. The knowledge came to me unwillingly, I hadn't wanted to remember it. But there it was. A year to the day. My body would have been much changed by now, marked by things I had not wanted to experience.

I never doubted that I had made the right choice, and it was not that I regretted not having the child, or a body that by now would have borne the traces of stretching, the accommodating, the darkening of nipples, the linea negra blooming down my abdomen. That wasn't the source of sadness.

It was sheer pity for myself.

Even then I could assess the events of the previous year and observe that it was all rather a lot to bear. Perhaps for a woman stronger than myself, everything might have progressed smoothly. But I was not strong. Taken together, the recent events of my life were of the kind that, in the past, might have made a weak woman hysterical. They might have made her take to her bed,

might have caused her to adopt the teachings of a spiritual leader, or have her committed to a regime of constitutional walks and water cures. I could see, in the mirror, and quite clearheadedly, that I had entered the dark waters all those months ago, and there I was still, clutching at lifebuoys, only occasionally able to emerge to the surface and take in the vast formlessness of the sea around me. I had the bruises to prove it, if nothing else.

I knelt down to retrieve my underwear from my bag. I had a dress folded in the bottom, and a nice pair of shoes. The dress covered up the bruises on my arms. I was meeting my mother and I did not want her to see.

I walked from Prince Alfred Park, up through an alleyway and towards the theatre on Belvoir Street where my mother waited on the corner, holding her handbag in front of her legs like a shield.

Your hair is still wet, she observed.

It'll dry, I said. I did the best I could.

The chimes that signalled the beginning of the play began to sound from the speakers in the corners of the theatre. People filed towards the doors. I followed my mother into the theatre.

The play was an adaptation of a Swedish playwright's most famous work. It had been updated for a contemporary audience, but the broad lines of the story had been maintained for history's sake. The play concerned two people, one rich, one not, who nevertheless felt powerless over their destinies, and who believed that in sleeping with one another they might no longer feel that way.

When my mother and I left the theatre she saw the male lead smoking by the stage door. She approached him. You were wonderful, she said.

Cheers, he said, and looked at me over her shoulder.

Come on, Mum, let's go.

Are you embarrassed? she asked as we walked towards Cleveland Street.

No, I said. But he just finished performing, he probably wants to be left alone.

It's always nice to hear praise when you've done a good job, she said. Besides, I like him, that man, whatshisname? I liked him in that show a few years ago on Foxtel, the one with the little girl who died. He seems lovely.

Maybe. I just see that actor around, is all. He's at the Courthouse a lot. Someone told me he got into a fist fight at the BP in Erskineville a few months ago. He beat up the guy pretty badly. Made a woman cry.

My mother shook her head.

The night was warmer than it should have been. A dry breeze rattled through the jasmine. Going to be a short winter, remarked my mother.

I guess so.

Here, your hair is drying funny, and she used her hand at the back of my head to scrunch a handful.

I pulled away. Don't.

She looked at me, her head on one side.

What is it?

You grow more and more like him, you know.

My father?

Mmm.

Don't say that. That's a horrible thing to say.

Around the eyes.

I pulled away from her. That I might be *like* my father was more than I could countenance. If I were like him then I too might have the capacity to weep on the stairs, crash the Mercedes, smash the windows, go off the rails more brilliantly and violently than I ever had before.

I changed the subject. Are you walking me home? Your car is that way, if I recall.

Don't complain. I'm your mother.

You realize I walk down this street in the middle of the night half the week, coming home from work.

I'll put some money in your account. Get a taxi.

It's a 25-minute walk. That would be a waste of money.

It would ease my mind to know you're safe.

I didn't respond. She put her arm through mine. We crossed at the lights on Cleveland Street and approached the ledge above which all the houses were built. Just then a scuffling sound started up from behind a green recycling bin left on the median strip, and we stopped in our tracks as an animal emerged from behind the plastic. The eyes of the animal glinted in the streetlight. It looked right at us. A sick misunderstanding had occurred. It's just a possum, said my mother. It's fine.

But it didn't move or run away. Instead the possum stared at us and seemed to puff up its chest. The animal advanced.

I dunno, it's pretty big, I said.

Shoo, shouted my mother, waving her arm at it. Go on.

The possum advanced once more. It opened its mouth to bare its teeth. There was a noise, suddenly, something between a growl and a hiss, but anyway a noise that announced her intention to attack if we came any closer. My mother cried out. We turned and ran into the street, across the road.

I've never seen anything like it, said my mother, standing outside the closed car yard of Sydney Prestige.

It must have something by that recycling bin it really wants to protect.

Possums are meant to be gentle. I've never seen anything like it. God, did you see her? She was so big. She was quivering with anger.

157

We stood across the street, looking at the recycling bin, but we could not see the possum in the darkness, we could not tell if it was still guarding the street, and so we continued to wait while the fire engines careened around the corner and towards Waterloo, heading south.

A FUMBLING at buttons.

Wait, I said. Wait.

What? The fingers pulling at fabric.

I. I. Jesus. I got my period this morning.

A rearing back. So?

You don't care?

No, and he was biting at my lips again, inching my underwear down my hips.

I excused myself. I ran downstairs, took off my tights and pulled out the tampon, leaving it wrapped in bloody tissue on the edge of the kitchen sink.

A moment of fear, should he look. But he didn't flinch. Didn't care. I expected there to be red all over the sheets. But there were no stains. It was as though everything were thinner, and diluted. A wetness.

Can I come?

Inside me?

Yes.

You can't. Yes. Yes. Come inside me. It'll be OK.

When it was over he lay back in bed and checked his phone.

I felt between my legs. A mess of pubic hair, his and mine. A butcher's block, I thought it might be. A minor murder scene. But it was not. Just skin. Just wet.

Then I noticed something, at the base of his cock. A globule of purpley-brown. Before I could take it from him, he reached down to his crotch. He took the clot of blood in his fingers, stretched and pulled the thing. It was animal, borderless, female. Soft and staining on his skin.

He wiped it on the sheets.

Then he kissed me, sat up and lit a cigarette. He leant over to set an alarm on his phone. What does she think you're doing tonight? I asked.

Working.

You don't feel bad about lying to her about any of this?

I love her, he said.

I turned away from him.

He told me, then, that he had spent the last morning, after I had gone, kneeling over his bed searching for strands of my hair. He could see them clearly in the bright light of the morning. Shapes of my body still there in the sheets. Smell on his fingers and his belly. He searched the pillowslips, the doona cover, the sheets, his clothes from the night before. He got on his knees and picked out the strands of hair one by one. When he had them all he walked out onto the balcony, opened his fist and threw my hair out into the street below.

Don't comb your hair in the bed, he said.

You pull it.

CATE SAT WAITING at a table outside the café on Redfern Street. She stood and hugged me as I arrived, the soft squish of wool-covered breasts pressing together. When she pulled away I noticed that long strands of my hair had attached themselves to the shoulder of her jumper. She didn't notice.

I asked whether she minded if I smoked. I said I had eaten, but in fact I hadn't eaten all day, hadn't eaten since lunch the day before. The idea of food was revolting to me. Chewed-up bread slid like mucus down my throat. As though while being so surreptitiously fucked it was necessary to reduce the functions of my body in all other respects.

I did not ask her how she was. She had a thin, wide smile on her face. I could see she was nervous about seeing me, so nervous she was almost shaking. She twisted the rings around her fingers, pulling them off and sliding them on again, and I could see, when she did so, the red marks she had developed through what was clearly a new nervous habit.

It is supposed that it took us until the mid-fourteenth century to begin using the word "fire" as a metaphor for the force of our feelings.

I asked Cate about her poetry. Was she still writing? This woman whose delicate prose was riddled, Lachlan had told me, with images of buttons and pearls.

The poetry wasn't working out particularly well, she said. She was working as a secretary to a friend of her father's, a dentist in Roseville, and getting sick of the trek back and forth from the suburbs of her childhood to the city of her adulthood. She

would try and write, she said, in her lunchbreak. But she was too loyal and trustworthy to work on her poetry during office hours.

I write at work, I told her. That's why it's such a good job.

Her phone vibrated beside her. She swiped her thumb across the screen and read whatever had been sent. He's at uni, she said, in Fisher. I might go and meet him there in a minute. It's not a long walk from here.

No, it's not.

"Where's the fire?" was standard American English by 1917. It was less common for English speakers in the Commonwealth to inquire about fire when people were in an obvious hurry.

He probably needs a break, she said. I'll take him for lunch. But God, he's been such a shit, lately. He probably doesn't deserve me being so nice to him.

Oh?

Just moody, because of his writing. And, I've told him, if you want to get up early in the morning to write that's fine, but can you at least go out onto the balcony so that I don't get woken up by your typing? I had a pregnancy scare last week, and it didn't help matters.

I thought you were on the pill.

I am. But, you know, things can go wrong. You're not on it, are you?

No.

What do you do?

Nothing. Get scared. I seem to be doing all right. I have my period right now.

By the mid-1860s, the expression "to play with fire" was in common usage. It was largely directed at badly behaved children

who meddled, risked disaster or treated a serious matter with carelessness.

I asked her how the opening night of his play had gone. She smiled. Nobody had come, she said. He went out drinking at the end of it all. She went home.

What's it about? I asked. The play.

It's mostly about his father, Cate said. It's very affecting. At the end I started crying. He never speaks about his anguish, but you could see it all. The loss. Are you going to see it?

No, I said.

The truth was that I was due to see it that night, when I knew she would not be there.

Perhaps because I was as young and half-formed as I was that year, I didn't really believe I had the capacity to affect Cate. It did not occur to me that I made her nervous, rather, I believed she was constitutionally anxious. Perhaps both were true. I was so bound up in the struggle to keep my head above water that it seemed inconceivable I might affect those around me in the way they affected me. Part of me felt guilty, part of me even liked Cate. But when I was with her I was jealous and, in the deepest part of myself, furious. For what I perceived as her happiness, her ease with the world. So I sat there drinking coffee, with all the calm of a behavioural scientist at the helm of an electric buzzer, knowing full well I had the capacity to cause her extreme pain, but having no real belief that anybody had the capacity to feel pain but myself.

You should meet him for lunch, I said. I'll come with you.

In the late eighteenth century, an experimental chemist interested in gas anchored a small boat in a stream. He strung a pipe

from the shore and set it up so that the end of the tube rose just above the water line. He conducted the gas upwards through the tube, and lit a match. He observed to his friends that "he had now set the river on fire". In the nineteenth century "to set the river on fire" became a common expression, used to refer to a remarkable and usually foolish achievement. By 1830 it was often used with the name of a river, and varied by locality. *To set the Thames on fire, to set the Hudson on fire, to set the Lachlan on fire*, and so on.

Our bill arrived, and I laid down money for the coffee I'd drunk. She had barely touched the hot chocolate. I think it's great that you and he are spending time together, she said, looking again at her phone. Twisting her rings. It's good for you two to be working through your problems and getting close. It's what I've been telling him for ages.

I crossed and uncrossed my legs, stringing my hand through my hair. My fingers came away threaded with bright red strands. They burned in the light. Cate startled, and her train of thought halted. Oh no, she said. Are you shedding?

No. What. Never mind. I always shed a lot of hair.

But not like that. That's way too much.

I untangled the hair from my fingers and tried to throw it quickly down onto the pavement, but hair doesn't take to being thrown easily, it sort of drifted there in the air, still clinging to skin and jumper sleeve.

Are you terribly stressed? she asked. You know you can lose your hair from stress? That job you do must be stressful.

Yes, I know. But I don't think it is. It's not that.

It's not normal to lose so much, she said again. She offered me advice: relaxation techniques, the benefits of not working so much, perhaps drinking less.

As she talked I remembered how hard he had pulled my hair back, how he wound the strands through his fingers and tugged as if my hair was a rope to hold onto, and I looked at her hair, very brown and smooth and sleek, and I wondered, doesn't he do the same thing to you?

IN THE MORNING I found it. Dead, and lying in the gutter. Somebody had moved it so that it would be out of the way of the traffic. I stood above the mess of fur and bone, uncertain about how much attention I should visibly give to the dead possum. I crouched down. It was impossible to tell if it was the same animal I had seen with my mother that night after the play. But she was, I was sure of it. I was close enough to touch her.

She was splayed stomach-upwards among gum tree leaves and cigarette butts. Something had pulled off her face. The nose hung loose and bloody by a strap of grey-furred skin. Ants swarmed in the red flesh. The possum still looked angry. Her mouth was fixed in a growl, although the teeth were smashed in and her jaw misshapen, hanging off her face. Broken, I supposed. I could see where the wheels must have crushed her, but it wasn't just a car that had caused the damage. Something else had got to her. The possum's pouch had been half torn-off. I could make out the wet pink of teats below, and her fur was sticky with milk and congealing blood. I could see no sign of her baby. The cars accelerated along the street. I stood up and took a step backwards. The men in the mechanic's were not watching, nor the people at the bus stop, no one was watching. Nobody would pay her any reverence.

The idea came to me then. To grind down my boot on her skull and break her broken teeth further, to tear off the pouch completely and expose the whole of the raw flesh to the punishing sky.

But I didn't.

I turned, and I left her there.

*

Before I was born, before they moved to the suburbs, my parents lived in a house in Enmore. My grandmother, when she came to inspect it, peered around at the lightless walls and the mould-catching cupboards. You couldn't swing a cat in here, could you, she said. Both of them young, my parents worked at law firms and made good money, the kind of money that allowed them to buy a house at the age of twenty-five, and the kinds of excellent drugs that could drive a reasonable man to wildness.

At nights when they lived in Enmore, my mother took the train from Circular Quay to Newtown Station and walked home. One night, during the summer, the little Greek ladies sat in the cement-poured front yards and old men watered tomato plants and kids squealed through open front doors. The heat was sticky. A group of men loitered at the top of the street. My mother saw them as she neared the corner. The house was in sight, my father's first Mercedes parked out the front. This was before he went off the rails, of course, before he smashed our windows, crashed the Mercedes, wept on the stairs.

That night, a man peeled off from the pack. He walked towards my mother. He didn't say anything, but he smiled. When he reached her, his right hand extended forward. His hand lifted up the hem of her knee-length skirt, and the man grabbed my mother between her legs. She didn't say a thing. The man smiled. He held on.

After what seemed like a very long time, she pulled away and heard the laughter of the other men loitering at the top of the street. It's just a joke, love, she heard one of them call out. She walked down the street towards her house, as though nothing had happened. The old ladies in the front yards didn't meet her eye, and the old men watered the tomato plants as though she wasn't there. She opened the front door and closed it and my father was inside, with his shoes off, reading in a chair, a rum

and Coke ice-cold beside him on the side table. She said nothing about what had happened. Because what could he have done? And wasn't it best to keep these things from the people we love? Once the damage is done what can anybody do?

MAEVE AND I STOOD side by side in the ladies' room. She pinned her hair into place and nodded to me in the mirror. We headed for the door. We were at the Courthouse. In a fortnight, Maeve would be leaving the country. She would live in Vietnam for six months, maybe a year, if things worked out. Teach English, perhaps. Her boyfriend had planned it, and for him she had deferred her law degree.

The noise of the pub rose up and broke around us as we nudged through the throng of bodies shouting their orders over the taps. Maeve left me, headed outside to the wooden tables on the veranda, and I stood in line beneath the healthy smiles of the Sydney Swans players erected on the walls, trying to control my breathing.

I wanted badly to be drunk.

On the television mounted in the corner of the bar, a news update flashed across the screen. Footage showed a man being escorted from a white van, up a staircase and through a courthouse door. Cut to the white van driving away from the courthouse at the end of the day. A woman in a black coat stood by the open gate, holding a sign up to the van's tinted windows. It read: May u rot in there.

Earlier that afternoon, I had listened to the radio playing in a café on Castlereagh Street during one of my breaks. A woman with an accent was speaking to the radio host. She was Dutch and she had been backpacking through Melbourne a few years earlier when she had encountered the man who killed the woman in Brunswick. Standing outside a pub one evening, she said, he had pulled up beside her and told her that somebody

was following her. He said she'd be safe with him. She got into his car and he sped her away. The man had lied.

Her voice was matter-of-fact. He was on me, the Dutch woman explained on the radio. I saw myself being killed. He could have done anything.

The Dutch woman got away. He hit her and he raped her, but he didn't cross the line of no return.

The radio host had not asked the Dutch woman about the apparently chance series of events which had led to her being trapped in the man's car in suburban Melbourne, nor her thoughts on why her mistake had not been fatal. I had wanted the host to ask the woman those questions, because I suspected that she would not be able to explain. How could she?

The man had been convicted that afternoon in a Melbourne courtroom. The articles I read on my phone between emergency calls explained that the man had sat in the dock wearing a dark shirt, his hair tied back, surrounded at all times by four prison guards. When the verdict was read, the judge had started by saying that the rape and murder were "savage and degrading".

He had chastised the man for telling the police "a farrago of lies" before admitting to what he had done that night in Brunswick last year. The articles described the man as "impassive" as he listened to the judge read the verdict.

The judge said that the man in the dock could have easily controlled the woman if he had wanted to. He was bigger than her, and stronger. The woman had fought back. She had threatened to call the police. And whether it was because the man found pleasure in hurting the woman, or he was afraid of being caught, he had strangled her there in the alleyway off Sydney Road early on a Saturday morning, and she was killed where she stood. "This

was particularly heinous," the judge concluded, "as you hid the body and were on parole at the time." The judge sentenced the man to life in prison with a 35-year non-parole period.

As I waited in line at the bar I kept my eyes fixed on the screen. The sound of the crowd was too overwhelming to hear what might have been said, but it didn't matter. It occurred to me that I was surrounded entirely by disinhibiting strangers, and it occurred to me that an anaemic with poor liver function who is in the midst of ordering her third drink of the evening would be in no position to fight anyone off if that's what it came to.

The line for the bar inched forward and beer wept into the carpet and I fingered the ten-dollar note in my hand.

When the man killed the woman in a laneway in Brunswick he had been on parole from prison. Years earlier, when I was still a child, the man had raped five different women in the southern suburbs of Melbourne, all prostitutes. When he attacked the five women in the southern suburbs he would park his car with the passenger door so close to a brick wall that the women could not escape.

The issue of parole had become a great topic of conversation in opinion pieces and the television news. The question being, would the man have been granted parole if the women he had raped years earlier had not been prostitutes? Is the rape of one woman qualitatively different from the rape of another?

Earlier that day when the sentence had come down, that question had been discussed again on the news broadcast silently above the tripartite desks and the phones. The dumbest fucks here had joined in. They had thoughts. They pointed out that there are different kinds of chicks. Different rules. It's just different, hey?

Because some women are asking for it, and a prostitute, they observed, is positively inviting it.

The news rebroadcast the footage taken from the bridal shop, the last known images of the woman before she died. We watched it again, all together, while we answered the phones. The men in the call centre noted that the woman on Sydney Road turned. She'd looked back. And she followed him just the same.

Once I got to the front of the bar I was squeezed between two tall men and ordered. It was only turning towards the corridor that I saw Sean, Lachlan's housemate, standing on the edge of the pack.

Hey, I said.

Hey. He didn't look at me, but ahead at the television screens over the bar.

Who are you here with?

Just some people from my doctoral programme, he said. He gestured towards a group of men wearing glasses.

I don't know them, I said. I don't really know what I'm doing here.

Right, he said. I scratched at the label on the bottle of beer until it began to peel off, to disintegrate. I was waiting for him to say something else. I wasn't sure how much he knew. I didn't know if he had noticed my sounds in the upstairs bedroom of his house. I was never quiet, except when I was leaving.

He looked at me then, with an expression of exasperation, because I was not going away. I don't know what you expect me to say to you, he said. I mean, what the fuck do you think you're doing? He shook his head. I just have nothing to say to you.

Outside in the courtyard people were huddled in coats and scarves under the outdoor heaters, dropping ash in the soil beneath the frangipani trees. Taking a seat at the long tables I took swigs of lukewarm cider and huddled beside Maeve. Her

friends argued around us. They were the kind of people who didn't expect me to speak much. Maeve peered at me. Should you be drinking quite so fast?

Why do you say that?

What about your liver? You said the doctor told you not to drink.

I don't know. I'm not drinking that much.

You look like shit. And what's this? She held up my arm and examined the thumb-shaped bruises wrapped around my wrist.

I pulled down the sleeve of my jumper.

Maeve let go. She got distracted as she argued with somebody across the table about the efficacy of the union movement. At the other end of the table her boyfriend bickered with another man. Why do all the women in Japanese porn look like they're being hurt? They look like they're being forced.

No, man, you're wrong. You're wrong. They like it. It's just that that's what men like over there. They want their women to act like they don't want it.

Maeve took a strand of my hair and smoothed it into place as she talked. I was afraid of her leaving. Her breath was warm on my neck, her fingers easing through my hair. I depended on all of her small intrusions of affection. In Vietnam it would be hot, and I would be lonely in Sydney without her.

You know that Pavement song? I asked her.

Which one?

"Darling don't you go and cut your hair."

She laughed. Yeah?

That's why I don't cut my hair, I said.

You're ridiculous, she said. Also, you're drunk.

When the Courthouse closed at midnight crowds of people exited the beer garden and progressed down Eliza Street towards the

173

seedier pubs on King Street whose licences let them stay open well into the morning. Maeve's boyfriend and a group of his friends disappeared into the dark of Camperdown Memorial Park, saying they'd be back in a second.

What are they taking? I asked.

I absolutely do not give a shit, she said.

I did not believe that Maeve and her boyfriend would be coming back from Vietnam in love. The fighting was constant. She couldn't stand the drug-taking, or most of his friends. And he wasn't prepared to move out of his parents' place to come and live in the parts of the city we lived in, neighbourhoods which he thought were dirty, and full of hipsters and too many immigrants. I didn't see how the two of them could emerge from four months at such close quarters and still find something redeemable about one another.

We stood on the corner of Lennox Street on the edge of the park. The Moreton Bay figs rustled and the sound of the crowds slowly receded. It was cold enough for our breath to form clouds. I lit a cigarette while we waited for the men to return from the cover of the trees.

I hate when you smoke, she said.

Hey, do you remember last year when we found those masks here?

Masks?

We were walking to a party somewhere near here in Newtown, and you found those three plaster of Paris masks of a man's face? Outside the door to the Courthouse. And just took them, because they were on the street?

Yeah, she said, why?

Do you remember we took them to the party, and they were so weird, these big white plaster of Paris faces? And then Cate showed up, a half hour later, and she walked in and saw them

and told everyone they were reproductions of the death mask taken of Ned Kelly after he'd been hanged? And we made fun of her when she left, because she sounded so fucking smug and convinced. Because somebody looked it up and Ned Kelly died when he was twenty-five. And these masks were all plainly of a man in his fifties, he was completely bald?

Yeah? I mean, I remember *you* making fun of her.

Cate was right, though.

About what?

They *were* replicas of Ned Kelly's death mask, those things we found on the street. She was right.

So? And looked hopefully into the dark of the trees to where the men might be.

I dunno, I said. I've just been thinking about it.

H E SAID, as he lay down, that there was a sick ball of stress in his stomach that he had been carrying around all week. He said the only time he'd felt like things were all right was right now, there with me. This is the best I've felt all week.

I touched his hair.

Did Sean say anything to you?

I mean, Sean says a lot of things to me.

About me, though.

No. Should he have?

Don't worry. No.

His house was empty, the doors to the balcony wide open, letting the light in through the silhouette of a forest, a stage prop he had acquired from someone, by means unknown to me.

You won't stay, you know, he said.

Stay?

Away. In America. You'll come back. The prodigal son always returns. Daughter, I suppose.

I don't know about that, I said.

The truth was that even then I had no intention of ever coming home. I wanted a warm, sunny climate far away from this one, a place that had nothing to do with me, and where there would be no history or memory tethering me to the land. I wanted him to ask me to stay. But in the list of wants that I could draw up and submit to a higher power, the desire to leave was far greater. The truth was that I wanted him to ask me to stay, so that I could have the pleasure of saying no.

I'll miss you, he said.

Which caused me to kiss him. Then we were grasping at each other. We took the clothes from our nakedness.

Don't scratch, don't scratch, he whispered.

One hand pinning down my hair, he moved on top of me. The other hand holding my breast. All his weight bearing down on my body. Streetlight poured into his room. We were sheened in sweat. One another's.

I scratched him anyway.

I didn't care how he would explain it. Red fingernail tracks down the plain of his back. Places where I had drawn blood. I didn't care. This was my back, I thought. Not hers, or any other woman's. I claimed it for myself.

I'm close, he said.

Come inside me.

Really?

Yes. Come inside me.

And he did.

That was stupid, I said afterwards. We shouldn't have done that.

In the morning we walked together towards the shopping strip on Erskineville Road. Be gallant, and come to the pharmacy with me?

Of course.

The pharmacist asked me to fill in a form. We sat in chairs by the end of the aisle, or, rather, Lachlan sat, and I knelt on the floor, using the chair as a writing surface. I hate having to take the morning after pill, I said. It makes me insane. I expected him to say, Well you asked me to. Because I had. But he did not. He reached out and stroked my hair.

I completed the form and handed it to the pharmacist. By the counter Lachlan fiddled with the aromatherapy oils and neatly stacked tubs of shea butter. What is this for? he asked.

To make you soft.

The pharmacist handed me the box and smiled. Take it with some food, he said. I know, I replied. This was the third time I had bought the pill in the last twelve months, since the procedure. It was always unpleasant, always embarrassing, but it felt necessary. The previous pharmacists had offered advice on safe sexual practices, had often spoken in condescending or concerned tones. But there was none of that when I bought the morning after pill with Lachlan. This time I had shown up with a man wearing a tie.

Thanks, guys, called the pharmacist, as we walked towards the door. He waved a friendly hand.

We sat down at a table in a café next door with a vase of small purple flowers between us. I said I couldn't eat. You should eat, Lachlan said. That's what the guy said. I nodded as he looked at the menu. He seemed happy, expansive, as I grew more and more anxious. What the fuck is za'atar? he asked.

I shrugged. Spices, and fingered the box in my lap. Thank you for coming with me to do that.

He smiled. It's fine. I'll write about it one day.

I suppose it didn't occur to him that both of us could write about it.

He ordered a toasted cheese sandwich. I ordered a muffin. I opened the rigid magenta box under the table, after the food came. I could only stomach one bite before I swallowed it down. One tiny white pill in an orange blister pack.

There. It's done.

It's all right, you know. This isn't a disaster. We're sitting here having lunch together, and it's fine. This isn't like before.

I picked at the muffin. It was dry, maybe stale. I didn't want it. Why didn't you do anything, last year?

What do you mean?

You never texted me back. When I went to the clinic. I told you I was afraid.

Why are you asking about this now? He pushed his hand through his hair.

What is it?

You never really wanted *me*, you know. You wanted an idea you had of me in your head. Some story.

No, I said. That's not true. That's not what happened.

But he was right, of course. What I enjoyed most about my affair with him, from first to last, was the comfort of the narrative arc. Because affairs never last, and that knowledge was, in its own way, reassuring. I wanted the comfort of his voice, the safety of the bell jar, but I also wanted the inevitable conclusion, I desired it like men desire water in the desert.

In the early evening, when we were sure that his housemates were gone for the day, I left. I made my way down the creaking staircase, and shut the dark red door quietly.

I stood for a moment on the narrow pavement, looking up at the green iron lace on his balcony and the stage forest and the shirts he'd pinned to the clothesline beneath the awning. I had to stifle an impulse to slam the gate. Because once I left, I felt untethered. As though I were suddenly adrift.

I had left hair pins all through his bedroom.

The street was strangely empty of people as I walked home. Green lights turned to red over the empty intersection. It was strange that Elizabeth Street should be so empty, I thought, when there were so many people in the city. And yet sometimes I was sure I could hear footsteps behind me. When I turned, there was no figure, but I was afraid to turn around the whole way. There was always the chance I had missed whoever it was in my peripheral vision.

The space spread out as the brothels began and the street got darker. I had always been wary of that section of Elizabeth Street,

the stretch between the Strawberry Hills Hotel and the late-night Lebanese restaurants on Cleveland Street. I wasn't afraid of the men who frequented the brothels. I was afraid of the angry man on the street who had been ejected from them. Of being the first woman he saw, of being the sudden second-hand object of his anger. And I wondered what would be left behind of me when I was gone. A handbag, a phone, hair pins? The fear is that you'll leave no trace. Or that the trace you leave won't be adequately apprehended, like salt plains and the smell of seaweed in the desert. It's important to leave clues, I thought as I walked. So that somebody can find you when you're gone.

CRACKS, FISSURES, TREMORS. The crockery was rattling in the cupboards. The glasses had smashed. Just past one in the morning when the centre was quiet and I had an hour left to finish my shift. Police in Ernabella. Can you spell that please?

The waves of pressure began deep below the surface, spread outwards and upwards, expanding, compressing and advancing like a snake.

The building is shaking!

Emergency police, fire or ambulance?

The building is shaking!

What state and town is the emergency in?

South Australia.

And then just dogs barking, yelling, something falling from a shelf with a thud.

Footpaths cracked. The bed inched across the room. The door swung off its hinges.

Emergency police, fire or ambulance?

Who do you call for an earthquake?

Later, seismologists would note that this, the third big earthquake in the northern part of South Australia in twenty-seven years, made the remote town most unusual. "Ernabella's seismic activity makes it one of the few areas in Australia to have experienced multiple large earthquakes in our recorded history," said the scientists. They promised to "monitor" the region.

I played with my hair and connected the calls. I didn't think we got earthquakes in Australia, I said to Pat. Is this normal?

Well, it's happening.

Guess so.

Emergency police, fire or ambulance?

You know, I said, after a ten-minute silence, there was an ancient Roman theory about earthquakes. Pliny the Elder said that earthquakes were an expression of the earth's displeasure about her violation by men. He thought that the land was like a woman's body. It wasn't even really a metaphor for him. The earth *was* a woman, according to Pliny. He thought that digging around in her, mining for gold or silver, made her angry. He said mining would lead humanity to ruin. Earthquakes were a warning that we had fucked up.

Pat sighed. Right. And who is Pliny, when he's at home?

Ancient Roman. Died in Pompeii. He saw Vesuvius erupting and went to investigate. Took a boat towards the volcano and ended up dying there, from the poisonous fumes of the volcano.

He went towards an erupting volcano rather than running away?

Yeah.

Well that's bloody stupid.

I MET CLEMMIE in Annandale late on a Friday afternoon, in the playground of the primary school. I still found it strange that she was a teacher now. That either of us was old enough, let alone responsible enough, to stand in front of a classroom and instruct children in language and maths and ethics. I still felt like I was essentially a child.

Clemmie said we had to walk the long way to the bus stop. She did not want to pass by the café on the corner. Most of the teachers bought coffee there in the mornings, but the week before when she had been drinking at the Vic she had run into the barista from the café, kissed him and ultimately fucked him in the back seat of her car. She couldn't remember his name. She didn't want to run into him and have to admit it.

Later, at the pub, after only one drink and half a plate of fish and chips, I found that I had to excuse myself to weep in the bathrooms. I wept with some confusion. A part of me was able to stand back and enquire what I was so upset about. But I couldn't come up with a reason. I had no idea why I was weeping.

When I returned to the table I found Clemmie had invited three Irishmen to sit with us. She asked me, quietly, why I looked like I had been crying. I told her it was the morning after pill, and the cascade of hormones, which wreaked havoc with my equilibrium. She nodded. But it worked, right?

Yeah, it worked.

Good, she said, and returned her attention to the Irishmen.

The next afternoon we would confer, and realize that while we had both slept with one of the Irishmen, we each thought ours had been named James. One of us was mistaken, but neither of us had taken their phone numbers, so we would never know.

I ANSWERED THE PHONE. Emergency police, fire or ambulance.
Shit, uh. Police! Um. Yeah. Police? 'Cause there's a snake
in the bedroom, see. Shit. And I have a baby. And I shut the
door. But.

Connecting to the police. What state and town is the emergency in?

Rockhampton! Queensland.

Connecting to the police in Rockhampton, Queensland.

Quickly. 'Cause, right, I'm standing on a chair but they can
climb, I think. Aw shit. Fuck. Is it black or brown ones that's
worse?

They are both bad news, I thought, but could not say.

When the call was over I waited for Maeve at the phone
beside mine on the tripartite desk to finish transferring through
her calls. I sat watching the television, a news segment about a
dodgy plumber, probably foreign.

What happened to you last night? We were all sitting around
in my backyard having a nice time and all of a sudden you were
gone.

I'm sorry.

You just took off. Do you even remember how you got home?

Sort of. Not really. I'm sorry. I went off the rails a bit.

I don't know why you're apologizing to me. I am neither your
conscience nor your liver. Emergency police fire or ambulance?
What state and town is the emergency in? Connecting ambulance
for Maryborough, Queensland. Do you want to talk about this
off-the-rails business?

No, I'm fine.

Oh fuck off. That's such a don't call me, I'll call you response.

I didn't mean it to be.

I mean, do you know you're drinking too much?

Only sometimes. It's just. Emergency police, fire or ambulance?

Maeve was correct in saying that I had begun to drink as though I were hoping it might kill me. Nights when I couldn't remember what I'd done, but my phone contained messages I couldn't remember sending, half-formed, desperate, misspelt missives from a woman half wild. Mornings when I would wake up in the half-light of my bedroom and spend the next hours asking somebody else, often Maeve, to explain what had happened to me. Sometimes I would receive flashes through the fog—a rear car door opening, a face across a table, fingers in my hair. But sometimes I got nothing, and then I would face down the formless, dark thing that lived inside me, the thing that destroyed story.

Blackouts happen when there's so much alcohol in your blood that your body stops being able to store new memories. The larger narrative of your life is there. But nothing new, when you're in that kind of state, gets incorporated into the framework. The right-now splinters away from your ability to record it. And so a person blacked out is living in the absolute present tense. When I drank my responses became more visceral, activated by the baser instincts. My inhibitions dissolved. And on those nights of blackout I could stumble down quiet, dark streets, invite myself into the back seats of cars, scream at the face across the table, enjoy the strange fingers playing with my hair. I could abandon the everyday project of my safety.

I'm sorry, I told her. I'll do better.

"It is impossible to imagine a more desolate region," Oxley wrote in his journal in 1817. "And the uncertainty we are in, whilst traversing it, of finding water, adds to the melancholy feelings

which the silence and solitude of such wastes is calculated to inspire."

Oxley was in a bad place. He was not of sound mind. The horses had died. Food had become scarce. They survived on bush rats and bandicoots. One night, when his men were starving, they managed to catch and kill a dingo. The party gathered together and roasted it over the fire, and although the men said it didn't taste too bad, maybe a little like mutton, Oxley retreated to his tent. He could not bring himself to eat it.

A dingo was, for him, an indignity too far.

One night in this hallucinatory nightmare he had wandered into, as the hope died and his dreams flailed, Oxley heard shouting and barking. In the distance, along the edge of the dark, he could make out the figure of a running man. The dogs chased after the figure. They attacked. It was the only Aboriginal man the party had seen in weeks. He was a man six feet tall, with a long beard, and "no arms of any kind".

T HE WEEKEND BEFORE Maeve left, we drove north and stayed overnight in a campsite somewhere near the mouth of the Hawkesbury River. On the radio the news discussed the likelihood that it had been "kids", by which they meant "boys", who had been responsible for starting at least some of the recent spot fires. We drove north through Ku-Ring-Gai, along the dark lightless roads where once I remembered the national parks service telling my mother and me to turn back. The bush we drove through had been burnt once, and had long since regrown. As we drove, Maeve remarked on how eerie it was, how dark and silent the country. There were stars, but no streetlights. Eucalyptus and ocean in the dark blue of distance. You'd get murdered out here, said Maeve.

When we arrived at the campsite the light had already faded and neither of us had the wherewithal to pitch two tents. We stopped after we'd assembled one, and prayed for a windless night. We opened a bottle of gin, and listened to the car radio with the passenger door open. We had decided that this trip was the thing we should do to celebrate my leaving, and hers.

We should go to bed early, she said, if we want to be up for the dawn.

Maeve slept in the tent but I preferred to sleep in the car. In the dark I could see the light upon the river. I thought the sound of the water would lull me to sleep, but stretched out on the back seat I couldn't get comfortable. My rolled-up cardigan made a poor pillow, and the sound of the cicadas was deafening. I watched Maeve in the tent from the car window. Making sure she was safe.

*

In the morning I was woken by banging and shouting. It was barely dawn, a thin blue light. The cicadas were gone, or muffled, perhaps, by the smacking on the windows.

I shot up.

Maeve was tugging on the locked door behind my head.

When I pulled up the catch she flung open the door and threw her arms around me. What's wrong? I asked. She was breathing hard. I thought you were dead, she heaved into my hair. In the tent she had only half-slept, and in the half sleep she had heard somebody come for me in the car. Lying there in the tent, she was paralysed, there was nothing she could do. She was stuck inside her own limbs. She was unable to cry out, or run to me. She came out of the paralysis shouting, unzipped the tent and came fast at the car. She was wearing only underpants and an old T-shirt, her bare feet in the eucalyptus dirt luminescent in the grey light. The Oaxacan heart on her wrist stood out sharply on her pale skin, as though to sloganeer the savagery of love.

A nightmare, I said. I stroked her hair.

I know, she breathed.

She opened the door to the passenger seat, crawled in and closed the door. She dozed while I lay back down, unable to sleep on the rolled-up cardigan.

In time, I edged myself quietly from the back seat and walked down to the water's edge. The river flowed east.

The river stretched out still and windless, the trees closed in. I wrapped my cardigan around my body. The tide was restless and dark. A cloudiness that was unappealing. We could not see the bottom. I remembered the stories I had heard, of the sharks that trawled the mouth of these waters. We would not be swimming. It was too cold. Too muddy. We had come up here for nothing, I thought. We had supposed that we would enact some kind of

baptism, some final rite of friendship before we both left. But we had fucked it all up. The sun had already risen.

Watching bodies of water is soothing, I told myself. Just watching it might be enough. Watching the tide is like watching something broken trying to make itself seem whole.

When Maeve woke we drove out of the national park and back to the highway. We rolled the windows down and as we approached higher ground the car radio began to pick up FBi and we began to see signs of different lives.

We stopped in a roadside McDonald's and brushed our teeth in the bathrooms. We ate hash browns and drank bad coffee at sticky tables. Children screamed in the car park and we listened to them instead of talking to one another.

H E AND I SAT shoulder to shoulder on a bench at the top of a hill with the entire city stretched out below us in the dark. A bottle of red wine passed between hands. Lachlan slid back, his legs spread wide. His hair was unruly and standing up in tufts. He seemed distracted, as though perhaps he didn't want to be there. And I wondered why he didn't want to be, since he was the one who had asked me to come out.

Are you OK? I asked.

Yes. Why?

I don't know. You seem. Something.

I'm fine. Are you?

Sure. I exhaled. I took a swig from the bottle.

Lately he had been telling me about the great loves and hates of Patrick White. White had listed them, once, in preparation for a portrait sitting. Lachlan had them pinned above his desk on the wall. White had loved reading, uncluttered landscapes, sex, whisky and the thought of an Australian republic. He had hated writing, insomnia, noise, motels, talkback radio, and "the overgrown school prefects from whom we never escape".

In turn, I told him about things I had written down in the notebook. I told him, for instance, that throughout most of history, Chinese scholars were obliged to study and commit to memory the Mandate of Heaven. The text, very ancient, justified the rule of the emperor. One could tell when Heaven had withdrawn its Mandate, for there would be a flood, a fire, an earthquake or a storm. Until the very end of the Empire it was standard practice

for the Emperor to issue an edict of remorse and self-criticism after a natural disaster befell the country.

Why do you know all of this stuff about disaster?

I just pick them up at work, around the emergencies. Fun facts.

Fun.

Interesting.

We're out of wine.

I guess so.

There's a pub on the corner down there, he said. Come on. We left the bench.

We can go back to mine?

I nodded, and followed him, lagging behind, keeping track of the back of his head, the stretch of his shoulders bearing back down the hill towards Newtown.

We made our way through the higgledy-piggledy of the smoke stacks and the rusty corrugated iron. You know, I said, passing through the shadows, when I was younger I would skip school and just walk around. I used to come to this park. I'd sit over there in the grass, reading Lawrence Durrell or Dylan Thomas or something. Hoping somebody interesting would speak to me.

He looked at me, with an expression that indicated he wasn't uncharmed, which I suppose was what I had been aiming for. Did they?

Speak to me? No, nobody ever did. Not about the books at least. I was very plain when I was a teenager.

The lights flashed red across my skin as we approached the neon sign of the pub across the road from the park. The smell of spilled beer was carried on the current through the open doors. Non-Stop Beautiful Ladies, read the sign in the blacked-out window. I don't believe that you have ever been plain, he said.

*

In 1951 Patrick White went out in a storm and slipped in the mud. There, on the ground, cursing God, he suffered a moment of ecstasy in which he at last apprehended the divine. But it was not just God he discovered down there in the mud. God was tied up with the man he loved. They were almost indistinguishable from one another. "My inklings of God's presence are interwoven with my love of the one human being who never fails me," White said. Manoly Lascaris, the love of his life, was the man who had saved him from loneliness. The worst suffering imaginable was loneliness. But, like love, God could only be apprehended in fragments, as "the result of a daily wrestling match, and then only by glimmers, as through a veil". There was both sting and salve to suffering, although, White observed, "I have always found in my own case that something positive, either creative or moral, has come out of everything I have ever experienced in the way of affliction."

A game of NRL played on the mounted televisions above the bar. There were sticky floors, pokies flashing in the corner, and tiled walls for the better resonance of misery. The non-stop beautiful ladies had taken their neon smiles and glitter and gone home for the night. The remaining clientele were by then all male, suffering in their loneliness at half past eleven on a Tuesday night.

A witchy shape of advanced age stood by the bathroom walls. She wore a long skirt and neat blouse, with a big carpetbag slung across her shoulder. She swayed a little. I watched her as Lachlan bought another bottle of wine from the bar. When she thought nobody was looking she grabbed what she could from the empty tables about her, angling everything down her jowly throat, but sort of sideways. I saw her leave by a back entrance while Lachlan counted out change. I had liked her and wanted her to stay.

Come on, he said.

*

In 1755 the city of Lisbon was destroyed. The ground shook, the buildings fell, the water trembled and broke its banks and drowned the unlucky. Shortly afterwards, John Wesley noted that it was clear that God had rained down retribution on the Portuguese because of their stubborn fealty to Catholicism. They had brought destruction on themselves. By his reasoning, God had chosen to punish Portugal for its idolatry, and who was Wesley, or anybody else, to send aid or prayers to ease the suffering He had meted out.

Lachlan and I spoke at cross-purposes, but there was a common thread I can now detect in our Fun Facts, our anecdotes. The world was cruel and beautiful, and we longed to have it justified. He, in pinning down the life of a man's mind in the unreadable prose of a doctoral thesis. I, by the sheer accumulation of information. We both supposed, deep in the most hopeful parts of our selves, that such projects might help us build a kind of life raft we could float on together when the flood arrived.

We stepped out of the alcove and walked down King Street, past the shuttered cafés and dress shops and the bikes chained to the wrought iron of rented terraces. By a yellow building that sold furniture by day, we took a left.

From a bench by the ornamental grasses a hand emerged from the darkness. It clamped around my wrist. I turned.

Because she was partly obscured by the long grass, I hadn't noticed the old woman from the pub as we had walked by. But she was there, looking up at me. Her fingers were very white and the blue veins bulged against bone. She was small. Her hair was escaping its hair pins and she sat with her ankles crossed like a schoolgirl in the front row of a class photograph. Her eyes were too big in her face.

Look at your hair, she said.

I smiled at her and said, Thank you. Lachlan hovered at my shoulder.

Titian. The colour of your hair is called titian, she said. Do you know titian? It's very rare, that colour. And oh, it's just beautiful. That colour. That's the right word for hair like yours. The artist, Titian, that's what it's named after. Because, see, he painted women with glorious red hair. Just like yours. She wouldn't let go of my wrist.

I felt Lachlan shift his weight from one knee to the other as he watched the woman speak to me. Her voice had the same frightened tremor as the women who called Triple Zero in the middle of the day.

Looking closer I could see the egg yolk dried in long drips down her skirt. She had fitted a button of her blouse into the wrong hole. It made the fabric gape just under her breasts, where I could see the edge of a dirty white bra and a stretch of soft flesh shot through with broken blood vessels.

Her grip tightened. She looked right into me.

That kind of hair signifies fire, you know. I nodded as she spoke. Lachlan put his hand on my arm and gently pulled me away, out of the woman's grasp. I smiled at her, as though to reassure her. She didn't blink. A smell of unwashed wool and beer floated in the air.

I can read your past, you know. Let me tell you.

But we were already walking away. Her voice rose. I had made her cross.

Charlatans and whores, the lot of you. Pack of bastards. Here, though. Listen to me. Titian? He painted Mary Magdalene with red hair. Because she was a whore. Ah, go on. You'll see. The future is coming and it doesn't look good.

We turned the corner and continued down the thin street

full of terraces and trees. I looked back. But I couldn't see her. There was only tall ornamental grass rippling in the wind and the yellow streetlights.

Christ, said Lachlan. You get a lot of attention.

There are many notable dead seas of the interior. There is, for starters, the Salton Sea, the incidental fuck-up of a 1905 irrigation project designed to connect the Imperial Valley to the Colorado River, which caused such high salinity in the water that the birds and fish began to die. If you encounter a dust cloud when near the Salton Sea, do not breathe in.

Then, too, there is the Aral Sea, once the fourth largest inland body of water in the world. But the Soviets wanted to grow melons and rice. They diverted the waters. Instead of a sea we now have the Aralkum Desert. Winds have lifted toxic dust from the Aralkum and scattered it across the globe. Scientists have detected Aralkum dust in the blood of Antarctic penguins.

Meanwhile in Africa, water hyacinths began to grow on Lake Victoria. The hyacinths spread like smallpox. Soon the fish below the surface suffocated. More than five hundred species were chased into extinction. Now boats float in fields of hyacinths. The lake is dead, and so are the fish beneath. But observers note that the corpse looks beautiful.

When he closed the door of the room he pushed me up against the wall, pulled my tights down to my thighs, put his fingers inside me. My knees gave out. Overcome by lust, or love, or both. An ill-fated lifebuoy, this figment of a man I've named for a hopeless river. You can't come inside me again. He covered my mouth with his hand. Our shoes were still on. There were no lights in his bedroom and I could not see the shape of the room around us. I want to be the reason you make those noises. He bit my ear

lobes and my neck. He bit my nose. I came, still pressed against the wall. We pressed against one another. Heaving. And wet. Everything wet, and engulfing us.

In his very last interview with a television crew from the ABC, Patrick White was asked, "How important is love to life?"

"It's all important—but not lust."

"What type of love is important?"

"Affection, I think. Yes, affection."

"Do you have any expectations left?"

"No. To die comfortably, to die in my own bed. Not in the bath."

I would like you to know that when I die, I would not mind going out in the bath. Bath, swimming pool, ocean. I don't care. I only ask that you please let the water take me.

FROM WAY BACK in the past we can begin to see things clearly. Zoom back. Take stock. Acquire some much-needed distance.

I want to show you my most treasured dead sea of the interior.

Look down now from this imagined space in the sky above the land.

Observe the vast sweep of history and time, and direct your gaze to the millions-past, the ancient times, the before-memory of this place.

See the way the desert ripples and wriggles across the landscape? The way the sand seems to swell and ebb with the sun? The way the brown seems flecked with light? Can you see the steady movement of the tide? This is no mirage or desert fever-dream. This is the Eromanga Sea.

The continent looks different, when seen this far back. More like an archipelago with a stripe of water separating east from west. There is no coral in the Eromanga Sea. Instead, the water is home to abundant fish and crabs, cockleshells and turtles. There are reptilian dolphins and crocodilian shapes crawling through the shallows, armoured fish, all forms of scaled, saw-toothed and cold-blooded biting things. This is sea monster country. But beautiful. Aquatic plants grow by the waterlines. Birds soar overhead.

Crank the dial and you can speed through the years by the million. Watch the sky fill with debris, blocking out the sun, watch the proto-crocodiles and scaly dolphins die for lack of light. Watch the years peel forward. Watch the ocean recede. As the water dries up the iron-rich soil erodes. An underground freshwater reservoir forms. It's as though the ocean sinks down,

below the surface. The Great Artesian Basin covers the same area as the long-lost sea like some subaqueous shadow. The Eromanga Sea leaves behind a dry red desert replete with opal, and hundreds of ghost-streams and poorly watered rivers that flow not east out to the Pacific, but west, petering out into the salt plains where once there was ocean. It still smells like seaweed out there. Sometimes there are swans.

But skip forward from the present moment, just a little. Watch the apocalyptic climate maps jump from computer screens and take their predicted form. The sea need only rise a few metres for the Great Artesian Basin to unbury itself. For the rock and sand and red gibber plains to become submerged once more beneath the sea. Fish will return. They will swim around the drowned branches of the mulga and the mallee and the saltbush shrubs.

Because Oxley wasn't wrong, exactly.

He was just 110 million years too late, and a few hundred years too soon.

WILDFIRE

THE YEAR I WAS ELEVEN, I received a book in an orientation package for the high school I would attend in the coming year. The book was a large, hardbound volume printed to mark the centennial of the Ladies' College, now School for Girls, and given out to every new student upon her enrolment. The book described the school's founding, the evolution of the grounds and pertinent pieces of history. Buried towards the end of the book, a small column of text detailed an incident that had occurred in the 1950s. The school grounds had once held a wing to house boarders, an old part of the campus now used for official ceremonies, interviews with the press and annual vaccinations. In April 1958, the book explained, a 29-year-old man had broken into the boarders' dormitory and abducted a fourteen-year-old girl. He had taken her to a nearby park, raped her and then stabbed her to death. Because she had screamed, and he had been afraid that she would report him to the police.

When I started high school, I realized that I was the only girl who had read the book over the summer. In those first weeks, I looked for traces of her everywhere. But I found that, outside the book, there was no memorial for the girl who had been killed in 1958. The boarders' quarters had been closed after a fire in the 1970s, but the structure was still there. I would look up to the tower sometimes, and imagine it back then, how quiet and frightening it must have felt to be snatched by a stranger in the middle of the night. Every day at lunchtime Clemmie and I would assemble outside the building where the girl had been abducted, to sit cross-legged on the old tiles where we dirtied our dresses. During all those years of segmented mandarin halves and forged permission slips we never mentioned her. I'm not

sure that Clemmie knew anything about the girl from 1958. But I thought of her often. I knew that, just as my home could be violated by burglars, I could not be kept safe from the world, not even at a School for Girls, formerly a Ladies' College. Not for all the long socks and blazers, or the neat hair, or keeping silent with strangers. You could simply disappear, and the only trace you might leave behind would be a mention in an old book. There wouldn't even be a memorial plaque. Just light, just grass, a hair pin, a memory, a handbag and a SIM card. If you were lucky.

I TURNED FROM PAT to answer the phone. There were sounds in the background, waves and the sea breeze and people calling out. The voice started panicking right away. Ambos. Oh fuck ambos, maybe the police? Fuck I dunno. My mate's being bitten by a shark he's still in the fuckin' water.

What state and town is the emergency in?

Coffs!

Coffs Harbour in which state?

Campbell's Beach.

Campbell's Beach in which state?

Fuck the shark still fucking has him fuck fuck quickly we're on the beach. It's fuckin. Fuck. Elouera Street? It's Elouera Street. Mate! It's gonna be OK!

Connecting to the police for Coffs Harbour, New South Wales. Please inform the police that you'll also need an ambulance.

The police answered, I read out the job number and hung up. I went back to speaking with Pat. We were discussing the alleged sexual proclivities of the youngest, virginal daughter of the Prime Minister. Sharks already, huh?

Yeah. Seems early for sharks. Although I guess the summer's already started. It's only October but it feels like January.

True.

Emergency police, fire or ambulance? What state and town is the emergency in? Connecting fire for Mount Macedon, Victoria. See, there's already spot fires starting up in paddocks.

Later that evening, on the Channel Nine news, a beach in Coffs Harbour flashed up on the screen above the phones. A nineteen-year-old body boarder had been killed by a shark at Campbell's Beach in Coffs Harbour just before 2 p.m. The

footage showed the emergency services trekking through thick bush to get down to the unpatrolled beach from the street above. That was all the information I could absorb from the silent television. They filmed the paramedics lifting his body through the bush on a stretcher. They had placed a white sheet around his form. They weren't hurrying to get up the hill. The emergency was over.

THE OBSTETRICS WARD of Prince Alfred Hospital was parcelled away in a building off Missenden Road gated by palm trees rustling in the wind. I followed the arrows along corridors of clean linoleum and glass walls. The doors were built wide to accommodate gurneys and the waiting room I eventually found myself in smelt like hand sanitizer and decay. I checked in with reception, sat with the other women and waited to be called. High windows built at the far end of the waiting room opened out to gum trees and the football pitch of one of the university's residential colleges.

The waiting room in the obstetrics ward was entirely different from last year's waiting room. No purple chairs, no *30 Rock* on the television overhead. There was no television to speak of. Sitting against the wall on a squeaky vinyl chair, a teenage girl held her round belly. A boy sat beside her, holding her hand, swaddled in baggy jeans and a Penrith Panthers cap. I judged that he was not old enough yet to grow facial hair. Across the aisle a sensible-looking woman in her thirties sat knitting the arm of a tiny cardigan while the man beside her swiped his thumb across the screen of his phone. I put my hand on my empty stomach and pressed down. I held a book open on my knees without reading its pages. Was it not odd, I wondered, that they put us all together in here?

I had almost forgotten about the procedure to implant the IUD until the hospital called to confirm the week before. After the doctor's visit, after the morning at the pharmacy and the single pill in the blister pack, I had made phone calls and received a referral to the hospital.

*

I had come in once before, three weeks earlier, for a consultation. During the consultation, I had met with the doctor who would conduct the insertion. She told me about research trips she had made to Mozambique, the public health initiatives she was involved in, the challenges facing women and girls in developing economies. She was tall, and clearly spoken, and I trusted and liked everything about her.

The gynaecologist had reassured me that she had done the procedure hundreds of times over the last twenty years, and she was convinced I was making the right choice. It was the most responsible thing I could do for myself, she noted, and I confirmed that I wanted to be responsible.

That morning, three weeks earlier, she asked me to take off my underwear and lie down on the examining table. She pressed down on my belly, checked between my legs, and pronounced me completely healthy.

This morning, sitting in the waiting room, I was sniffling. I had had a bad cold for three days and had been lying in bed watching the sun stream through the windows. I hadn't eaten anything, although I had been told I should.

The corkboards above the vinyl chairs in the waiting room were emblazoned with messages. Warnings about soft cheese and alcohol and shellfish, health notices listing the early symptoms of pre-eclampsia, and missives from the Australian Breastfeeding Association. Nobody has the right to tell you that you cannot feed your child. A list of ten reasons to breastfeed your baby. Warnings about smoking printed in indignant type. Remember that what you put into your body, you put into your baby's. The message board seemed to suggest that the universe was full of danger, and women were too thinly screened from its evils, too porous to the world.

A nurse came to fetch me. I followed her sensible slacks and Elizabeth Taylor helmet of hair down a fluorescent corridor. I was left by the door to the office and told to wait. I had already taken the painkillers. The doctor had told me it would hurt. Not as bad as labour pains, a little more than period pain, she had said. I sat by the door under the humming light and I pressed my nails tightly into the palms of my hands until I could see the little half moons etched in red. I took another painkiller, just to be on the safe side.

When the nurse called me into the room the doctor was still looking over her notes because she had forgotten who I was. Her manner was pleasant, but she was running behind schedule and did not look me in the eye. She asked me if I had collected the copper IUD from the chemist and I handed her the long white cardboard box I'd been keeping for weeks in my bag. Whatever was in there, I couldn't believe that it would fit inside my body. I didn't have any clear idea of what was inside me, let alone its shapes, its size or what it could accommodate.

Behind a screen I rolled down my tights and underwear and placed them on a chair. I pushed my dress up around my waist and inched along the surgical table, adjusting the loose, starchy sheet that shifted as I moved.

The doctor pulled back the curtain then and began to work. She asked me to lie down, and it wasn't as cold as I thought it would be. She placed my feet in stirrups. She pressed on my pelvis, and all across my belly, just to check. I stared at the ceiling. This is going to hurt a little, the doctor said. I felt something clamping me open, maybe a finger. It didn't hurt.

And then it did. A deep pain that went up my spine and landed in my throat, a pain that threatened to jolt me out of my body through my mouth. Galloping spasms. I whimpered. The nurse and the doctor spoke quietly around my hips, they were

switching implements, but the fingers kept moving inside me and the pain kept gushing up my back and the whimpers kept coming. The nurse asked if I was all right. I said I was fine. My fingers clutched at the edges of the surgical table and screwed the loose sheet into tissuey balls. Something wasn't right.

The doctor pulled her hand out of me.

It isn't working. Your uterus is too narrow. I'm worried that if I push it in harder I could puncture the uterine wall. I'm sorry, I'm not comfortable proceeding any further.

She began cleaning up the instruments. I could see the copper thing in her hand, the long sharp end of it coated in blood. I had not realized that there would be blood.

Do you want me to try again? she asked.

I shook my head. The doctor's face had taken on an expression of extreme frustration. I could not see where she put the thing, now that it was of no use.

This is only the fifth time in a twenty-year career fitting hundreds of these that I haven't been able to do it, she said.

I felt sorry for screwing up her track record, as though in a vital sense I had failed her. She told me to lie still for a minute as she disappeared behind the screen.

Sometimes fiddling around with the cervix can trigger fainting, she called.

I lay still, looking at the ceiling tiles. The spasms of pain had begun to subside. When I sat up I looked down between my legs. There was blood on the sheets. Very bright. In the blue surgical bucket below, on the ground, where my hips had been, there was more of the stuff. Thin, a rich red, the same colour as my lipstick. More blood than I'd ever seen come out of my body. It was trickling down the plastic sides, making dripping sounds like the last of the rain falling from the eaves. I watched my shadow move on the surface of my blood in the bucket.

When I emerged, fully clothed again, I sat across from the doctor as she explained that what had just happened was a statistical anomaly. Very rare. But there was a new model from America, it was due to be introduced here in maybe six months' time. We could try again then. If I were still in the country. If that was what I wanted. But the point was, we just couldn't go ahead with any of the options currently available to me.

Do you feel all right? she asked.

Yes, I nodded. I'm fine.

She examined my face. You're going to faint, aren't you?

Oh no, I said. Then I fainted.

When I came to I was in a different room in a white hospital bed. The nurse was there, folding a towel.

Oh good, you're awake, she said. She was worried about you. You know, I would have tried again. Those things are very expensive. And you've already paid for it. I would try again.

She paused for a moment, as though remembering the protocol she was meant to be following.

But that's just me, she said, folding roughly. Your decision.

I lay on the bed, observing the ceiling. It seemed to glow and pulse as though it expected me to understand its meaning. But I wasn't capable of understanding anything. My mind appeared to have detached itself and sailed away from my body.

I remembered, then, that I had told nobody about the appointment, and as a consequence, nobody knew where I was.

When the nurse returned she handed me juice and forced me to sit up. What's your job? she asked. I sipped the sugary liquid through the child-size straw. The room pitched and my hearing dimmed. As though the volume had been turned down on the world. I lay still.

I'm. Um. I'm a writer.

Good, she said, piling the towels one on top of another in her arms. You can write about this.

From the door on the opposite side of the room she turned and said, You stay here till you feel better, that's what the doctor says. We have lots of patients. Not many beds. But you stay here. Other patients will wait, I guess.

She opened the door and closed it loudly.

When I sat up my body left my head behind on the pillow. My shoes were on the floor, my bag on a chair. I waited a moment while the texture of the walls and the ceiling glowed and pulsed. I put my shoes on.

I opened the door and walked very carefully down the corridor, past the noticeboards and reception desk in the waiting room and out into the glass walls of the hospital at large. I looked for an exit sign. I could feel blood thick and wet slicked between my thighs. I would need to throw away the tights that I was wearing. Nobody seemed to notice me leave. I walked slowly by the shuddery palm trees of the hospital's entrance, down Missenden Road towards the chicken shop and the motorcycle café on Parramatta Road. I stopped on the corner and looked at the bus stop. It occurred to me that I might well faint if I caught one. And then, I suppose, wind up back in hospital. And who would I call? My mother? I didn't want to talk to my mother about this. I didn't want to talk to anybody. I was humiliated. I had tried to do the most responsible thing I could think of. I had tried to look after myself. And my body had physically rejected all my gestures at attempting to vouchsafe its protection.

It was the middle of the day. The sunlight cast a tepid blue across the six lanes of traffic and the roar of the cars.

I hailed a taxi.

The cab driver wanted to chat. He was Greek, he told me, and he played in a mandolin band on Thursday nights in Drummoyne if I was ever interested in hearing some old-fashioned Greek mandolin music.

You're coming from the university?

Yes, I said, for simplicity's sake, and because it was easier to lie to strangers. I don't feel well so I'm going home.

He nodded and was silent a minute. I was overwhelmed by the sheer number of sounds, by the air conditioning and acceleration of trucks and the voices of the Radio National news bulletin.

What about your boyfriend, is he at the university too?

Yes, I said. The cab driver smiled at me in the rear-view mirror as he drove me past the auto body shops and university research centres towards home.

Well, he said, he must be a lucky man. Pretty girl like you, I know any Greek man—I'm Greek, did I tell you that?—any man who had his head about him, he would be after you in a minute. If it was me, I wouldn't let you out of my sight.

Quietly, looking out the window at the curve of the road and the kebab shops and the brothels, I began to cry.

IT WAS THE MIDDLE of the night when the pain began. Cramps rolled through my abdomen. A rising tide of pain. Nothing would halt them. I curled myself around pillows. I got up and went to check the medicine drawer, but there were no painkillers in the house, only Band-Aids and disinfectant and expired anti-nausea pills.

Bleeding.

Blood seeped into my underwear. Enough to make me worry. Because why was I bleeding, and what could have gone wrong?

I trembled. Had the cold worsened perhaps? Had I contracted something worse? What punishment was this?

My temperature rose. The street lights shimmered and lifted. Fever took hold.

Sirens careened out of Cleveland Street and headed south. They are coming for me, I thought. I knew, with absolute certainty, they were coming for me. The bats were conspiring in the trees and the man in his bathrobe was opening its folds beneath the grapevine, and the fruit from the mulberry tree was infested with baby snakes, whose venom is more dangerous because they cannot control their impulses.

Sirens.

*

I waited for the waters to rise and cover my salt plains, waited for the stretcher to bear me away, the policeman to hold me down, the fireman to douse my flames. Every siren was personal, because the border between world and self had been—it was now clear—washed away in the flood long ago. I was swimming in it. All things were wet.

Every siren was for me.

I slept.

And when I slept, I dreamt of snakes.

When I awoke in the morning there was a circle of dark blood beneath my hips, but I didn't get up or change the linen. The fever was gone. I pulled the blankets around my shoulders and rolled over, feeling as though I had been beaten. As though I had been punished for I knew not what, but that I surely must have done something to deserve it.

The next day I wrote on an empty page of the notebook a list of things I thought I needed: to quit my job, to go to the consulate and apply for my visa, to book appointments with the dentist, the dermatologist, a different gynaecologist and the hairdresser, to drink less, to take iron supplements, to use condoms, to get another STD test, two bottles of wine, Marlboro Reds, milk chocolate, a new dress, new books, sleep, a new pencil, need need need.

B LOOD LOSS. It's nothing too serious, the doctor noted. And your blood pressure isn't quite as low as it was. You're clear of the chlamydia. I'm still not happy about the bruising, but you're otherwise healthy. And what will you do if you fall pregnant again? she asked as she screwed the cap on the vial of blood she had taken from me.

I don't know, I said. I don't know.

You'll need to do something, she said. What kind of contraception are you using now?

I'm not.

Well, you know that's not good enough.

I did not reply.

I can write you a prescription for the pill, since you're going away shortly. I know you don't want to take it but it might be the best option.

I can't try an IUD again?

I wouldn't recommend it, after what happened.

I don't want to go on the pill.

I'm going to write you a prescription anyway. Just in case. She scribbled out words on the pad in front of her, the spiky indecipherable handwriting of a doctor who'd been doing this a long time. Practise some responsibility, she said, handing me the piece of paper.

I nodded. I told her I would figure it out.

ONCE I HAD A PAIN in my ear so great that I couldn't sleep or hear. The earaches began shortly after my mother and I left the house on the edge of the national park, when I was four years old, and we were living with my grandparents. During these earaches, which continued intermittently for several years, I had the persistent sensation that my head might simply explode. Even in those moments when the pain seemed to abate, I knew it would come back. This was because I could hear a rising sound in my ears like a wave drawing back and pausing before it stands, crests and crashes down upon the shore. I understood, then, that I could control nothing. Over time, the earaches stopped and I forgot.

At a certain point during the end of the year I am telling you about, after the two pink lines, the heart monitor, the anaesthetic, the pale green hospital gown, the pain, the bleeding, the fainting, the fever, and the blood tests and blood pressure cuffs and the blacking out, I remembered. My body could not be made to behave. It disdained all methods of prevention and protection. I could still hear the wave pausing before the crash.

These months before I left Sydney helped convince me that the improbable was probable. The earthquake could hit even a country without earthquakes. The car could veer and hit me. The fire would flash down the promontory and burn my house down. There would be a man at the door. He would be a conman, a swindler, he had a knife in his pocket and in his mouth. Phones ringing. Sirens. Simple as that. The environment was merely the outer equivalent of my inner reality. Or perhaps it was the other way around.

I HAD TOLD HIM I couldn't bear touching. I was still in pain from the failed IUD insertion, more than a week later. Still tender. And so we drove north. Parked in a lot by the road with only wilderness either side of us, administered by Ku-Ring-Gai Chase National Park.

There's a place to swim, through here, I said. You follow the path downhill about half an hour. And then there's the Basin. Our school used to take us every year before the summer holidays began.

All right, he said. If it makes you happy.

We walked. I did not tell him about the week before, the failed procedure, the fever or the dreams. Instead I told him about William Mulholland, the bringing of water to the American West, about "there it is, take it", arrogance and greed.

We set out along the path. The morning was hot. All I wanted was to swim. The path was narrow, and I walked ahead of Lachlan, chattering, complaining of the heat. Gum trees loomed above us. The undergrowth was dangerously dry. Ready to catch light.

When he had not responded to my chatter for some time, I turned around and looked back. Lachlan was standing far back on the path. He had stopped walking long ago. He did not move. I began to walk back towards him but he held out his hand. Hold on, he called out.

Something rustled.

After a few moments, he proceeded down the path towards me.

Why did you stop walking? I asked.

Because there was a snake at the edge of the path.

There was?

Yes.

When I was there?

Yes.

Why didn't you tell me?

Because I was afraid of it, he said.

What if it bit me? I asked.

Well it didn't, did it?

We continued to walk. I slid my hand into his. And thought about what it must have looked like, through his eyes. Seeing the snake emerge onto the path, stopping, and watching the woman walking on into the distance. Letting her go. And waiting for the snake to depart.

T HE FIRST TIME I saw my father after we had left he was slumped in the driver's seat on a Saturday morning. A car accelerated up the slope of the driveway and I rushed from my place on the gold filigree carpet to the space between my grandmother's curtains. Lace. Because, she told me, if God didn't want us to spy on our neighbours he wouldn't have invented sheer curtains. We stayed with my grandparents for three months after we left, before my mother eventually found the house in Ashfield.

I looked out the window between the lace curtains. My father was stopped in an unfamiliar car beside the camellia bush. Just sitting there. A white streak of happiness flared through me. I shouted out, jumped from the curtains and ran into the entryway. I got up on my toes to reach the doorknob, but the hand of my grandfather caught me by the tail of my dressing gown before I could even get the knob firmly in my grasp. His hands lifted me up, put me back in the living room and rolled the sliding door across the entryway with such a roar of force it almost muffled the shouting. What the fuck does that bastard think he's doing, showing up at my house?

I heard the front door open, loud voices on the veranda, the rise and fall of angry accusations without being able to decipher any individual word with clarity.

I watched the shapes of my family argue through the frosted glass. The television continued to broadcast Saturday morning music videos, the sanitized ones that Rage was committed to playing when children might be watching: Ace of Base, Kylie Minogue, The Cranberries.

The kettle whistled on the stove. After a little while the figures and their voices retreated inside from the veranda, and moved

away from the frosted glass and into the kitchen. The tone of my grandfather's voice still signified rage, but the ferocity of his objections sounded like it might be diminishing. I sat in place beside the electric heater I was not allowed to touch, swaddled in my dressing gown. The ancient television flickered.

Fifteen minutes later the door slid open, rattling on its rollers. My father walked through it. My grandfather followed behind him, smaller, withered, defeated. He was allowing a visit, just this once. My mother took me to her old bedroom where we shared her bed and she put me in a dress. She seemed to shrink from my father as she passed me over to him by the front door. It troubled me to see her so afraid. I swung my head back and forth between them but I couldn't, then, understand why she looked at him like that.

Not here, she said.

My father was driving a different kind of car. He had a tattoo on his left bicep that was new as well. Only a month or two had passed since my mother had left him for the final time, but things had visibly changed. The upholstery in the new car smelt like damp and chlorine, and there were clothes and boxes piled on the back seat. A woman's cardigan I'd never seen before. Cigarette butts stubbed out on the dashboard. The radio stations were programmed strangely. Triple J came out where Radio National was meant to be. "Darling don't you go and cut your hair," sang the radio. I took the sentiment very seriously. I would be well into adulthood before I realized that Cut Your Hair was not a serious song.

My father drove east, towards the beach, even though it was much too cold for swimming. We passed over unfamiliar hills, through eastern suburbs I had never seen before. He turned the radio down and spoke to me as he drove. I listened as the car travelled through shadows and late-autumn sunlight, past the

red lights of Darlinghurst, the barbed gates of Centennial Park, the exposed concrete walls of Bondi Junction. I listened to my father's voice—the dux of his year, Oxley's lawful descendant, the golden son who was never wrong. I listened to that voice in the car as he attempted to explain his version of events. Explain why he had been absent, why he was going to move away, why I mustn't listen to whatever it was my mother had told me he had done. Do you understand? he asked. And I nodded. He could have told me anything. I would have believed him. I believed everything he ever told me.

He parked on a hill at North Bondi and walked across the street to a café that looked out to the sea. He bought me a chocolate milkshake and a cheese sandwich. I had thought I was hungry. The air was cold and salty and whipped against my face. I did not eat the sandwich, and when we left the waitress asked me if there was something wrong with it. I shook my head, but I did not speak. Across the road from the café was a park with a whale-sized mosaic fish. It had a hole in its belly. I crawled inside and my father sat there on the bench by the swings, waiting as I lay curled up in the cold dark belly. It was quiet and riskless in the fish.

When he called me out there was sand on the knees of my tights and the elbows of my jumper. We took a winding path down to the beach. The sand was deserted, although the life-guards had erected the red and yellow flags to show the safe part of the water. Surfers paddled outside the flags. The waves roared over the rocks.

At the very end of the beach there was a concrete pool built into the sea wall, filled with the high tide's salt water. I didn't like ocean baths. Earlier that year I had seen a news story that scared me off them. In the baths at Palm Beach, at the very edges of Sydney, they had discovered a long, yellow-bellied sea snake

curled up in the murky depths of the water. A storm had washed it in. My mother assured me that a sea snake was extremely poisonous, but their jaws didn't open wide. They had to bite you in the spaces between your fingers, between your toes, to do you any harm. For years I swam with my hands in fists, thrashing through the water as though I were punching it.

I walked beside the mural on the rock wall, tracing the curves of the blue and brown sea creatures. I cannot remember how we got from the corso to the ocean pool, or where my father stood. Wouldn't he have been watching me? All I could see ahead of me were the waves breaking on the rocks and the black straps of my shoes tracing out the edges of the pool as the wind whipped around me.

The wind came. The water surged. I fell in.

I went under.

Wet wool, wet tights, shoes heavy with water—they all drew me down into the cold. I could hear my heart beating in my ears. There was salt in my nose. I beat at the water with my fists. I was floundering. Trying to fight it. But the water was bigger than me, and stronger.

I began to be afraid.

Then there were arms around me. My father caught hold of my body and took me to his chest. He hauled me out of the water and onto the concrete ledge where the creatures in the mural smiled down at me just as they had a few minutes before. We were both dripping. I looked back into the murky water, not understanding how I had come to be there. I held on to my father.

It's OK, darling, he said. It's all right. Everything is all right now.

That was when I began to cry.

*

Six months later the summer had arrived and my father had made good on his word. He had moved to Melbourne. He had another tattoo and he had taken the new car with him when he left. He had a new girlfriend, who the cardigan belonged to. She was twenty-three, English, seven months pregnant, she had a nose ring.

On the weekends of that summer, the first summer without my father, my mother woke me up early and drove us north to Palm Beach from our new house in Ashfield. On the sand I would hop from foot to foot as my mother tried to restrain me, rubbing sunscreen into my skin as I focused on the water. I wouldn't go near the ocean baths anymore, for fear of sea snakes and drowning, but the sea, to my mind, was different. It was each time a kind of christening. I ran into the water and I wouldn't leave. I was never scared of the cold, the bluebottles, the seaweed that gathered in clumps on the sand. The ocean took me in like I belonged to it.

My mother would sit on the sand watching me, always protective, always telling me I swam out too far. She asked me please to keep between the flags. When I told her I wanted to live in the water she dismissed the idea out of hand. She didn't like that I seemed to prefer being alone. She didn't like the thing she could see winking to life. Because she knew there was safety in numbers, that you have to swim between the flags, knew the kinds of dangers posed by girls who become women in a country where the land is not easily tamed. When the girl looks like she might not resemble someone else's vision of Eden, she winds up looking like just another girl who's asking for it. Because she wasn't what you thought you'd been promised. My mother knew that women have to hold up their end of the promise if they want to keep themselves safe.

*

By then I was all she had. We were gone.

When we left, we left in the middle of the night. Everything we had was packed into the back seat and the boot. She wrapped me in a blanket and drove. She had twenty dollars in her purse. We stopped, once, at a 7-Eleven on the side of the highway, where she bought Dairy Milk bars and a Kit Kat that she handed to me through the window. She didn't let me look at her face. When she drove she kept her eyes fixed on the road. I sat in the passenger seat still swaddled in my dressing gown and watched the darkness and the green road signs hurtle past the windows, announcing the kilometres remaining to suburbs further south.

My grandparents were waiting in the driveway when we arrived. Hard-faced, no smiles, no words. Just sounds. Sobbing. Rage. In the light streaming through the open door of her childhood home, I saw my mother's face, only for an instant. The darkness blooming around her right eye. The finger-shaped bruises beginning to form around her neck. The blood that had dried in the scratches on her arms. Everything that had been done to her was marked on her flesh. But there were no tears. Her eyes were dry.

I was lifted by my grandmother's shivering arms, taken down the corridor into the bedroom and put to sleep on the eiderdown. But a few hours later I woke up in the creeping light of the spare room and I didn't know where I was. I panicked because I couldn't see my mother. On unsteady legs I walked to the window and peered out through the sheer curtains.

I saw her from the back, standing out there in the driveway, looking down the slope to the cul-de-sac she hadn't known as home in sixteen years. She was barefoot, her hair piled on her head, holding a half-smoked cigarette by the hem of a big red jumper and looking at something out there in the dark. Currawongs were calling. She stood there for a long time,

smoking, as though she was waiting for something. She was beautiful. When she turned and came back into the house I didn't make a sound. She hadn't washed the blood off. Everything was visible, still.

I lay down on the strange bed. A cold, cyanotic light crept across the carpet. The wallpaper was gold.

But that's wrong, I thought. That doesn't make sense. My mother doesn't smoke.

S PRING HEATWAVE, said the *Guardian* in the morning when I checked my phone. Hottest day on record expected. Dangerous fire conditions. The winds were up, and a dry heat was cresting.

I left the house and walked to work. Even though it was early in the day, the heat was stunning. Bare shoulders. Smouldering pavement. A foreboding too-blue sky. At the traffic lights I watched the water I had spilled from my bottle of Mount Franklin seep back into the asphalt without a trace. Sweat rolled down my back. It was reassuringly cool in the air-conditioned atrium of the Telstra building. I scanned into the call centre and already I could hear it. The heavy traffic siren. The phones ringing.

I took one of the desks in the middle of the room. Outside in the park, elderly Chinese women had umbrellas up to protect them against the sun. European tourists sunbathed on towels laid out in the grass. On the television a sofa full of fake-tanned women discussed their thoughts on Miley Cyrus. Calls came through. Crashes on the M4, heat stroke inland, overnight break-ins just discovered, the sound of gunfire at the end of a cul-de-sac. Outside in the street the high winds caused the City of Sydney flags to whip around on their poles.

Somewhere in the country, the burning began.

The first panicked calls began around half past ten. Calls from Marrangaroo, Bilpin, Zig Zag. In nearly every case, the beginning of the fires looked the same. A smouldering turned into flames. Flames raced across dry grass. Husks of trees caught light, shuddered and lifted. Leaves like sandpaper. High winds pushed the flame forward, the enemy of property and annihilator of possession. The fire came over the mountain. It embraced

whole trees and homes and hillsides. The calls came thick and fast. Smoke, the voices said. Flames at the end of the street. Red glow on the horizon. Spot fires. Spot fires. Spot fires. There goes the shed.

Yeah, looks like the school is on fire, not sure if youse already know.

Hi, yeah, I'm home studying for my HSC and my mum's gone out but the fire brigade just came round and told me to evacuate but there's a fire already burning three houses down so like I don't know if I'm still meant to leave?

Look now. I've called four times and why aren't you here my garden is on fire.

Fire. Fire. Oh heavens. Fire.

Well, I'm in Parramatta, but is it possible to get the fire brigade to go out to my house and check on it, in Lawson? My texts aren't getting through to my wife.

An ambulance, dear, my husband has asthma.

What the fuck is taking so long don't you jokers know there's a fucking bushfire?

Awwww shit.

Over the voices on the phones I could hear the roar of flames, the crack of falling branches, the hiss of cinders in the air. The bark burned off the trees and flew like bullets. It sounded sometimes like I was receiving calls from a battlefield. Houses that had been safe when people left for work were gone two hours later. Through the tall glass windows of the office I could see that smoke had clouded the city. Everything in Sydney was red.

On the television above the desks I watched the breaking news on Channel Nine. News crews had flocked to the scene. The old railway at the top of the Mountains went up in flames. The Premier held a press conference. Helicopters hovered overhead. The fire had breached containment lines, said a spokesman for

the RFS; it was burning out of control. Everyone sheened in sweat and smoke. Wet patches under the arms of their business shirts. And I sat there in the office, watching the television as I listened. The calls kept coming. They kept coming.

Connecting fire, Lithgow.

Connecting fire, Gwandalan.

Connecting fire, Springwood.

Connecting fire, Winmalee.

Connecting fire, Catherine Hill Bay.

Connecting fire, Yanderra.

Connecting fire, Bargo.

Connecting fire, Lake Munmorah.

Please wait, the fire brigade *will* answer.

I'll try another line, please stay on the phone.

Please wait, the fire brigade *will* answer.

I understand. The fire brigade *will* answer. I'm trying another line.

At five I logged out and fled the building. But being outside didn't make me feel better. The city smelled like smoke. The heavy air altered all perception of clarity. I walked along Elizabeth Street towards home. The 7-Eleven seemed to loom into the street and the brothels creaked and the music issuing from the open door of the kebab shop was more like a wailing. There were no birds. And I could feel the sun before I saw it emerge from behind the smoke. Peculiarly illuminated against the blue of the sky, blood red. There were sirens, from all directions, everywhere in the city.

On television a few nights later, I would watch a United Nations official say that, while the direct link between the fire and climate change had not yet been established, what was clear was that heatwaves—which were increasing in both frequency and intensity—would contribute to the overall catastrophic fire risk.

She chided the Prime Minister, who had stood in front of a press room and announced that "these fires are certainly not a function of climate change, they are a function of life in Australia."

In my bedroom I opened the window and the smell of smoke filtered into the room. I propped the window open with a piece of wood and climbed out so that I was sitting on the window frame with my legs hanging down over the awning. The walls of the house scorched my skin.

I sat watching the street below. The heat of the bricks radiated against my skin. After a little while, a window of sky appeared between the tendrils of smoke and smog. It was relentlessly distant, and blue. As the night dipped in, great clouds of flame burned along the horizon in the west. We could all see it was out of control. Nobody needed the Rural Fire Service to confirm it. There was a horrible brittleness to the leaf litter, and crickets, and the sirens.

I looked directly at the paperbark tree across the street outside the mechanic's. It would take so little to catch light. For all of it to go up in flames. And would that be so very bad?

I could smell the smoke in my hair.

IN A STATE of sustained emergency, a chicken will play dead. In 1646 the scholar Athanasius Kircher observed that a frightened chicken would become utterly paralysed, "as if, despairing of escape through the fruitlessness of her motions, she gave herself up to the will of her conqueror." A toad turned upside down will likewise appear for all the world as if she has been paralysed. A goat will seize up and often keel over completely. A possum will begin to leak a foul, green fluid.

But humans cast into a prolonged state of emergency will tend towards more subtle physiological changes. Blood volume will increase, potassium will shed itself in the body's excretions, the immune system will stand down its battalions, and the brain will unwind. The mind doesn't distort reality necessarily, but its memory will suffer. Because the more a stressful memory is recalled, the less accurate, and the more prone one's brain may be to puncture holes in the narrative that we have convinced ourselves might freeze the melting snowcaps of our memories.

So is it enough to say that I don't remember, now, how it ended? Not precisely. There are holes. My recall has suffered. I remember not the beginning of the end, nor the hours afterwards, but certainly the moment of crisis. Is it enough to say that it was on Elizabeth Street, in the dark? Enough that it was three beers and a bottle of red wine and then Jameson, quantity unknown. I have flashes that emerge bright and appalling from the blackness, but not the ending itself.

*

I remember the toilet that didn't flush in the pub. The stumble from the cab and onto the kerb as I opened the door onto Elizabeth Street. I remember playing Nick Cave songs in my bedroom, and the feeling of his hand holding my face when he sat on the bed, in the curve my body made. I remember being in the hallway outside the bedroom, and asking him to stay when he told me he would not.

I remember that I told him that it hurt.

I remember lighting a cigarette. The streetlights. The squeal of the bats. The way the heat of the night engulfed the street. And that I shivered regardless. And I remember that I hated that body. My body. I hated it for shivering. I hated that my mind was not divisible from its form. I hated that both mind and body had caused me pain. And that somebody could want the form of the body but not the quivering thing inside. I remember the grief of that thought, the sheer, pathetic weight of it as it struck me. It's something everyone knows, of course, in the sober, rational light of day. But it hit me, in that wine-smeared present tense, as something heartbreakingly sad.

I remember him standing there beside me, smoking his own cigarette. I remember trying to communicate the weight of that feeling, in words that seemed entirely insufficient.

I remember that he said something, although I do not know what it was. But I can remember the way that he said it. Because for the first time in a year and a half, it didn't feel reassuring. There was no Home in his voice, no swollen rivers, no refilled water tanks. There were sea snakes in the storm surge and glaciers melting. It was the voice of a man from the Sutherland Shire,

who spoke like he had gone to Oxbridge, who kept a framed portrait of Patrick White above his bed, and who had promised me nothing.

I remember wanting him to comfort me.

I remember holding my hand above my head and slapping it loudly against his face when he would not.

I remember the bloodboil of fury. The cries as I hit his back. His arms. His face. A knee in the stomach. Tear at the hair. As I smacked and clawed at him. Teeth. Spit. Wailing. I remember that I wanted to bring him to his knees. He pushed me away. He turned.

And then blackness.

I WALKED HOME from work in full sunlight. The tourists sunbathed on towels in Hyde Park. The jacarandas were in bloom. I stepped through the patches of mushed purple on the sidewalk, and barely saw Cate waiting to cross the road outside Central Station.

Hey, she said. Reaching out to me.

Wow, hey. Hi. What are you doing here?

I'm having coffee with somebody on Crown Street. What are you up to? When are you leaving?

Soon. I just booked an appointment at the consulate for my visa. Should have it next week. My flight is booked. I'm moving out at the end of the month. Which, also, if you know anybody who would want to live in my house, let me know.

That's exciting. That's. Yeah. How have you been? How's Lachlan?

How's Lachlan?

You. Oh, you don't know? We broke up. Two weeks ago.

Oh. No, I didn't know that. I haven't seen him.

You haven't?

No.

Why?

I don't know, I said. I shifted my bag from one shoulder to the other. When did that happen? Breaking up. You guys aren't speaking, I take it.

No. Barely. I mean, I saw him for a second last week. I went over there to pick up some stuff. And he was so cold. You know? He just stood at the door holding it open while I collected my things. And there was a girl there. In the kitchen. I'd never seen her before. And then I walked back down the hallway, and I was

looking at him, trying to get something from him, you know, just something. Some acknowledgment. But he just held the door open, and he wouldn't look at me, and he didn't even say goodbye when I left.

I'm sorry, I said.

What about?

Don't worry, it's fine. I'm sorry about all of that. He, um. Well, you know what he's like. He was never very good at being *good*, in the end, I suppose. He's not good with other women.

Women? I thought it was just one. Just her?

Oh. Yeah. No. Um. I really don't know, Cate. No, I don't know.

And she was weeping. He gave me chlamydia, you know.

Oh. No, I didn't. I didn't know about that.

I should go, she said.

I hugged her. And walked on towards home in a blaze of sunlight.

The thing was, she never did find the red hair in his bed, she never saw the hair pins.

CLEMMIE HAD MOVED into the Marrickville house six months earlier. Everyone save salesmen and Jehovah's Witnesses entered via the back door, accessed along a cement path down the side of the house and the back garden. The garden was where I found her. Wearing the nightie she had slept in and a pair of gumboots, she was standing in the soil of the vegetable patch, trying to protect the tomato plants from the sun and the insects by wrapping them in grey netting. She wiped her hand across her brow and left dirt smeared across her skin. Hey. Fuck, it's too hot for this, she called out. The heat radiated up from the river at the bottom of the garden, into the cement courtyard with the plastic chairs and into the old bricks of the too-big house.

Clemmie emerged from the garden and walked towards me. Too hot to hug, I said, and she nodded with relief. She took her boots off and left them by the door. It didn't bother her that she hadn't seen or heard from me in nearly a month. Inside, we opened cold cider from the fridge and lay across the brown velvet sofas in the living room, sharing the stream of the standing fan by the windows. To pass the time we watched movies about disaffected teenagers in the Midwest from the '80s. Isn't it weird that it's going to be winter where you're going? she asked.

Not really, I said. I don't think they have winter there.

Oh, yeah. Two weeks left, though.

Twelve days.

The stream of the fan blew the hot air at our bodies.

When the sun set we peeled ourselves away from the wet velvet and into Clemmie's car. She applied blue eyeliner in the rear-view mirror and drove barefoot, with her platform sandals kicked to the side of the accelerator pedal. We drove to Paddington, with

the windows down. In a park that had been built on the old site of a women's hospital we found a collection of Clemmie's friends, a mix of art students, drug addicts, climate activists, tall men with shaved heads and tattoos. A blonde man with big calves pulled an Irish girl into his lap, and the rest of us sat in a circle on the grass. Cockroaches crawled up the walls of the white terraces. A girl jumped up and ran around the park like an aeroplane. There was no breeze, only air that drew thick and close around my body.

We walked back into the city. Bottles were passed among strange hands. The lights on Oxford Street streamed by. Clemmie and I let the others go ahead of us and told them we would catch up. In the dark of a laneway by broken wood fences Clemmie took two pills out of a ziplock bag containing ten. She gave one to me and handed me the warm mixture of vodka and lemonade she had been carrying around in her bag.

We walked to a tequila bar. It was dark inside, and packed with bodies. Girls standing by the walls rolled their hips to the music, solemn, balancing margaritas with stiff wrists. But we left before midnight when the liquor licences expired. The queue for the Soda Factory was long and the door fee at Oxford Arts Factory was twenty-five dollars. The group splintered. The others caught a cab to Marrickville. Clemmie and I went to the Abercrombie.

Rhythm, barely music. Bass that I felt in my collarbone. People moved against one another, just to touch. Sweat dripped down skin. It mingled with the beer spilt from jostling hands. The management had put industrial-strength fans in the corners but they didn't do much more than circulate the air. But the Abercrombie was familiar, and the beer was cheap.

I felt my dress wet against the skin of my back. Somebody twisted my hair in their hand and lifted it in a knot to bare my neck. I felt lips kiss me, and the cool air. Clemmie beside me,

handing me a drink. I held her to me and ran my hand through her hair. She was prettier than me, or differently pretty. I loved her strange shoes and her openness. We moved into the surging mass. I danced. Clemmie reached out to circle my waist and played with the neckline of my dress. My love for her expanded as the pill progressed through my system. I couldn't see my feet. There were plastic cups and puddles of beery sweat on the floor. I moved with the music.

I could see a man progress into the edges of my vision. He was all in black, with hair the colour of sand, and a shadow of blonde beard. He leant over and shouted something into my ear, about dancing, either that he wasn't good at it, or I was. Really, it could have been anything. He asked me what my name was, and where I'd been. The music was too loud. I cupped my hand and yelled my name into his ear. He put his hand on my waist and drew me backwards into his body, pushed his crotch into my back and slid his hands over my outline. I made eye contact with Clemmie and shrugged as if to say sorry. The circle of people closed ranks, jutting me out of it now somebody had claimed me.

The man with the sandy hair leant down and spoke into my ear. I could feel his stubble prickle on my skin. When I fuck you, he said, I probably won't last very long. But I can do other things. With my fingers and my tongue.

What makes you think you're going to fuck me?

Well I'd like to. He slid his hands up to my breasts and held them. The hands campaigned southwards, to the hem of my dress, pulling it upwards as though testing just how far I could be unclothed. He turned me around to face him. I tried to kiss him. But he didn't want to. Save it till later, he said. We're never going to see one another again after tonight. Everything can wait. It was nice being clutched at, as though my body served a function to someone other than myself.

He said he was going for a cigarette. I could come if I wanted. We walked through the pub to the door and turned right outside, to sit on a grey concrete ledge built into the new development. The letters glowed bigger than my body. Cars streamed down Broadway. Above us the buildings soared out of their scaffolding. The flower-covered skyscraper was right above us. A breeze sent shadows of fernery flowing across the pavement. It was as though the city had stopped being able to hold back the wilderness, and Sydney had returned to some formative jungle. There were flowers growing from the thirteenth storey.

I hate that building, I said, not looking at the man.

In the streetlights I could see he was golden from the sun. He was older than he had looked in the pub. When I asked he said he was thirty-two. He was rolling sloppy cigarettes and licking at the edges of the papers. I asked him if he could remember my name. He shook his head. He didn't ask me to tell him again.

What do you do? I asked.

He said he worked in the mines out near Kalgoorlie. Three weeks on, three weeks off. Isn't that difficult? I asked.

He raised his voice. Nope, he said. I'm rich. I come back to the city and get fucked up then go back and work. It's fuckin' great.

I did not know what they mined out near Kalgoorlie. I didn't really know what was of value in the ground, what resources were booming, what was making him rich. There was a rush for something, I knew that much. Or, maybe the boom had peaked and we had already entered a national decline? I didn't know. Didn't care. Fuck the nation. I knew only that Pliny had said you should not violate the body of the earth by mining her for what she kept safe beneath the surface, for she would lash out, eventually, in fury. The man beside me on the concrete ledge had emerged from the desert's red emptiness and from what I could tell the boom and the cash hadn't done him any good.

He stamped out the last of his cigarette. I don't want you to ask any more questions, he said.

I nodded. It seemed like a peculiar thing to say, but at the very least he was honest.

We went back inside. I'll get you a drink, he said. I pushed through the crowd to Clemmie and she took me in her arms.

Lights. The swell of the sound. Limbs soft and performing precisely the right gestures. We clung to one another, hugging and holding hands. I love you, she said into my ear. I'm going to miss you so much. She put her arm around my shoulders and stroked my hair with her hands. I kissed her cheek.

I had all but forgotten the man. But then I felt a hand on my waist, and he was back. I thought you'd gone, he said. I shook my head. I noticed that there was space in the bar now, people were leaving. It was two in the morning.

The man from the desert kissed me. I kissed him back for a few minutes. But my heart wasn't in it. I didn't like him touching me anymore.

That's OK, I said. You know, I think I'll go home.

The man said, Don't. He sat down in a booth opposite the bar and pulled me onto his lap. He was bigger than me, and I didn't want to hurt his feelings. He seemed too drunk to get really upset. No, I said. I'm going to go home. Having made myself clear, I stood up and walked away from him towards the exit.

Clemmie was kissing a blonde man in the middle of the dance floor. He's German! she shouted at me as I passed her. She waved. On Broadway I walked a few steps towards the pedestrian lights. I wanted to get a cab. I wanted to go home. And then an arm was whipping me around, an angry face. Where are you going?

He had run after me.

I'm going home, I said.

Let me come.

No. He held tightly to my arm. Let me go, I said.

Come home with me, he said.

No.

Why? Jesus, this is the worst thing that's happened to me all week. Come on, just come somewhere with me.

I don't think it's a good idea, I said. He pushed me backwards and pressed my body against the vomit-coloured tiled walls of the Abercrombie Hotel. He put his hand up my dress and groped. That hurts, I said.

Somebody walking by shouted, Get a room.

He kissed me and I kissed him back, as a sort of consolation.

Don't, I said, I don't want to. This is stupid. You don't even know my name.

I do.

I'm going to go home. He loosened his grip and I broke away. I hailed the nearest cab. I shut the door but the cab driver paused a moment to calibrate his route and the door flung open. The man was sitting beside me.

Get out, I said.

He didn't reply.

Get out. You're not coming home with me.

I was afraid that if I got out he would follow me. I considered what might be best. It occurred to me that if I got out quickly by my house, at the lights, before he realized, I would be safe. He didn't even know what suburb I lived in, let alone which house. I just wanted to go home.

The driver took off and I leant across to speak to him. When I get out, please don't let this man follow me. I don't want him to come with me.

Neither the driver nor the man beside me acknowledged what I had said. In the back seat he pressed his hands between

my thighs and I let him, as we got closer to Cleveland Street, where I would run.

When the traffic lights turned green I flung open the door. I didn't bother to close it. I ran up Elizabeth Street, past the bins and the shrubs and the patchy vegetation on the ledge, up the steps to my house. I clutched my keys in my hand, pressing one between each of my fingers. At the door I fumbled. The big old-fashioned silver key for the security door slid out of my hand and dropped to the floor. I bent down to retrieve it and heard running steps. I hadn't been fast enough. He was running up the steps towards me, he was at the door. Get out, I said.

Just let me come inside, he said. He gripped my arms and tried to kiss me again. I had made a horrible mistake. Somewhere along the line, I had made the wrong decision. He was bigger than me, and stronger.

I began to yell. Get out, I don't want you here.

Shut up, he said. Calm down. It'll be all right, just open the door.

Can't you take no for a fucking answer?

Then he grabbed me by the hair, held my head close to his. Be quiet, he hissed, veins and tendons bulging in his throat.

He pulled me by my hair into the dark of the shrubs on the ledge. All the vegetation in which he could hide me. The mango, the mulberry, the fig trees, the soil so polluted and wet and soft that when he pushed me down and my hand reached out to catch my fall I felt as though I were penetrating the flesh of the earth. The winds were up, the leaves lashed above me. A storm was coming. He yanked at my hair. I could feel it strain against my scalp, feel the strands breaking. You're a prick-tease, a fucking whore, he said.

Then I screamed.

*

Titian, the woman in the grass had said all those weeks ago. *The future is coming and it doesn't look good.*

Then we were flooded with light.

In the doorway stood Paul, in his boxer shorts, half-asleep. What the fuck is going on? he yelled. Don't touch her. Get away from her.

The man from the desert let me go. He stumbled backwards. Sorry, man, I didn't know, he said to Paul. She didn't say she had a boyfriend.

And he was gone, running down the steps.

I flew past Paul and into the hallway.

Paul called after him, Fuck right off, mate. Keep running.

He slammed the front door shut and locked it.

I burst into tears and fell back against the wall.

Jesus Christ. What the fuck was that? Are you OK?

I sobbed. I covered my face with my hands. Why did you do that? I said.

What?

I don't need protecting. I was fine. I was dealing with it myself.

He looked down at me. He shrugged and walked away, down the corridor and into his room. Yeah, sure. You're dealing with everything yourself.

I'm sorry, I called after him. I'm sorry. I stood up straight and watched him close the door. I stood in the dark corridor. Thunder struck in the distance. I stood there, among the cobwebs and creaking and mould. And then walked in the dark to the end of the house, to the bathroom.

The bathtub was filthy. Orange mould still growing along the edges, unabated. I wiped it down, turned the water on, undressed, got in.

*

Outside, the storm approached. The window rattled and a gust of wind shuddered through the bathroom. The shower curtain inhaled inwards, pressing wet and clammy against flesh.

The weather came in.

Wind and trees and leaves entered the bathroom. Thunder and dry lightning struck, but as yet there was no rain. I was safe in the water.

I put my head under.

My hair floated around my head, great chunks of it broken, and the scratches on my arms stung and the dirt and blood wept into the water along with the dead leaves, the mud, the wind rattling and trembling in the bathroom, and outside a branch crashed, a siren rose in the distance, but I was safe.

In the water I was safe.

THE FUTURE IS COMING AND IT DOESN'T LOOK GOOD.

O K. Let me tell you about the future.

Best-case scenario, the two-degree spike in temperature causes the oceans to rise five metres.

Look.

Watch what happens:

First, the water pushes up into Sydney Harbour, along the sunken streams, and into the suburbs. Flooding submerges low-lying beaches. Bondi is gone. So is Cronulla. The Parramatta and Cooks rivers spill their banks. The airport descends beneath the waters of Botany Bay.

Rising seas flood the sewers and warp the pipes beneath the ground. Sandstone slopes crumble like cake into the lukewarm tea of the Pacific. Before long, the salt water leaking into the soil starts to sluice away at the pavement above. All the Body Shops and Oportos and JB Hi-Fis renting space in the basements beneath the Queen Victoria Building and Martin Place begin to flood. After a while, the supporting beams buckle. Hyde Park caves in and becomes a lake.

Water city. Island continent.

This ruined Eden.

As the seawater gets into the soil, the wooden structural beams of all the old terraces in the inner city begin to rot. As the wood decomposes the trusses collapse. The walls lean to one side. Eventually the roofs fall in.

The seeds of pampas grass and crofton weed lift in the wind

and take root along the new-look waterways. Birds do the rest of the work. Soon, shoots of sticky weed and fountain grass have taken root in the cracks in the bitumen. The cracks get wider as the weeds grow taller. The roots of the paperbark trees and Moreton Bay figs, untended by the City of Sydney Council, grow out of control and split open the pavement. Pink and purple weeds flourish. Morning glory scrambles up the walls.

Down along the Cooks River and Botany Bay where the shipping yards and industrial parks have at last gone quiet, corroding petroleum tanks and neglected power plants leach lead, mercury, cadmium and zinc into the soil and the water. The nuclear reactor at Lucas Heights is safe enough from the rising oceans, but it's in the direct line of the fires.

Because the extremely hot days dry out everything faster now. The city may be soaked in the rising seas, but fire season starts earlier.

Turn your attention to the empty oven of the great red centre. In that place where our forefathers once stood feeling so breathless and melancholy and oppressed by all that vastness, the hot air builds up. Low-pressure systems moving along the cookie-crumb coast of the Great Australian Bight suck the furnace south-east, down and out across the mallee scrub and the grass plains and towards the blue mist, the ocean, the main attraction of the city coasts. A few weeks of that, and the heat has dried up everything. The soil is dry, the air is hot.

The accumulated leaf litter makes the centre of the city just as susceptible to fire now as the rural fringe. Eucalyptus leaves pile up in quick-burning tinder all across the ground. Their oil disperses in the air. A blueness cloaks the city.

Then dry lightning strikes and the land flames up.

Once alight, the bark on the eucalyptus breaks free. Carried by the wind, the burning embers fly through the air, extending

the fire front. The sky fills with smoke and then it goes black. Carbon monoxide from burning plastic makes the air toxic to breathe. Oxygen is sucked from the air. This causes a roaring sound. The trees turn black, crack and explode.

The fire encroaches upon the city. Flames race down Parramatta Road and Broadway and the Western Distributor and make their way towards the harbour.

If it's bad enough, the fire can produce its own weather system. The pyrocumulus is very like the cloud that follows the detonation of a nuclear bomb. It can reach the edge of space, throwing pollutants into the upper atmosphere. That smoke plume spreads out across the Pacific, towards Asia and the Americas, wreaking havoc on Los Angeles, Tokyo and Santiago.

The fire burns out, eventually. In the winter, the more frequent storms pummel the skyscrapers that haven't burned. The charred remains of metal topple over in the high winds, knocking each other over one by one. Sulphur-crested cockatoos, lorikeets and kookaburras make their nests in the broken windows of buildings. Lizards and possums nest in the drywall. Vinyl and aluminium sidings peel off and lie bleached of colour in the sun. Within a few years, vegetation sprouts in the ashy ground. New growth rushes in. Lantana climbs the sandstone, roots splinter the cliffs, and the wilderness takes hold.

THE FOLLOWING AFTERNOON, I packed up my room. I piled all my things onto the bed and bookshelves, and in the glare of the midday sun I walked down to the old hardware store on Redfern Street and bought sugar soap, a new sponge and a pole to reach high places.

At home, I poured the sugar soap into a bucket and washed down the walls. Every scrub of the sponge against the plaster broke apart old dust, cobwebs, pollution from the street. All of it trickled away. I washed until the walls were clean and almost completely white. I moved the furniture and did not bother moving it back. The removal team coming the next day would see to all of that. When the walls were clean I put the clothes into large plastic laundry bags, and began to stack the books into boxes.

I pulled the bed away from the fireplace and began to clean it out. The empty white space was covered in dirt. I listened to a shifting and scratching, up there in the bricks. And then with a sudden movement I ripped the cardboard from its place. A stream of disintegrated newspaper clippings and feathers and dirt heaped themselves onto the plaster. I tore up the cardboard and flipped it into one of the garbage bags sitting by the door. I looked at the fireplace and knew that I was done. No more.

I sat the cleaning spray down on a box of books and closed the door and descended the staircase of the house I was leaving.

I went outside to sit on the staircase leading down to the street. Night fell. A man set out wooden chairs in front of the art gallery. A Mercedes driver yelled at a mechanic across the street. I went walking. I waded through the people on Cleveland Street smoking outside bars. The traffic was thick and moving rapidly. A group of girls laughing together didn't see me, and

knocked against my ribs with their elbows. The cars screeched by. White and red.

A dog barked at me with wet yellow teeth, and through the doorway of a pub I saw three sad-drunk men sitting at the bar. Each alone, chin down, clutching at warming pints. Pop songs soundtracked their sitting. "I got a love that keeps me waiting", "Let's make the most of the night like we're gonna die young", "You'd better run, better run". On Redfern Street I passed a woman with her head hanging. Her underpants were strung around her ankles and she was squatting against the wall of the Centrelink office. She rocked back and forth on the balls of her feet, her eyes fixed on nothing in particular. Her knees splayed out, her arse close to the ground. I watched her. It struck me in this light that she was filled with some kind of pheromonal strength, the same strength that a wild animal might possess. All flesh and blood and breath.

A long, thick stream of piss hissed out of her body and trickled along the ground. At last, when she was done she wiped herself with her hand.

I might have felt disgusted, or even afraid. But I didn't. Instead, it felt more like relief. She stood up, hiked up her under-pants, and continued on along the street. I watched the woman walk away, and understood. We are meat, and flesh, and we are liable to scar. I was an animal, just like her.

The night got quiet.

I kept walking.

But there was a dread singing through the wires strung between the telegraph poles, in the breeze off the water and floating in electromagnetic waves beaming across the sky, a dread directed by forces I could neither see nor touch but which seemed as palpable as government, as humidity. The dread moved in the inconsolable vowels issued by passing cars and the twisting

bodies of bats moving across the sky. I stood at the corner of Regent Street and closed my eyes, trying to play games with the dread. I stepped out onto the tarmac. My body understood that it was dangerous to close my eyes and walk blindly across the street, but a second person existed inside the body, one that walked up to the danger and licked it, touched it, embraced it. When I opened my eyes the world was just the same, nothing had changed, no car or lightning or knifeman had come for me. The city was still a small and insignificant place on a stretch of shore in the far-right corner of the map, a city nobody remembered, or cared to pay attention to, a place that I was leaving. A cat outside a chicken shop. Trains rumbling below the street. Emergency. Phones ringing.

IN THE SECOND-LAST WEEK of November, when the jacaranda blossoms were beginning to rot on the pavement, I caught a bus to Coogee and walked across the hill and down to Gordon's Bay. There had been storms and torrential rain the night before, and trees had fallen through roofs in Kogarah. The storms had made everything strange. Cockroaches crept along the footpaths, moths besieged the street lights in the evenings, the cicadas screeched. The heat rose up in radiant waves from the bitumen, and everything was wet. Nobody was sleeping well. At night the storms rattled the paperbark trees against the mulberry and banana and palm, and in the dark rooms, in the curtained light, it seemed like the din and noise were beckoning you outside into the downpour. Just to witness the spectacle. The morning was sticky, but the sky was flawless, and the water in Gordon's Bay was clear. It was my last week in Sydney, and it was my birthday.

The morning was still early. I walked along the boat racks to get to the flat rocks where a body could stretch out flat on a towel. The storms had washed a scum of trash and mounds of seaweed onto the small stretch of sand. It was tangled together with chip packets and bottles of beer, milky condoms and bloodied Band-Aids. Nobody swam there. You had to walk further out onto the rocks and dive off to swim. I stepped slowly over the waterlogged planks of wood, barefoot. I was watching my feet. Then I saw them.

On the rocks, in the boat racks, in the seaweed, bobbing at the edges of the sand. Everywhere. The dead bodies of birds. Their grey wings jutted out. They were large, but windswept and battered-looking. The birds hadn't yet begun to smell.

Further along the rocks the bodies dispersed. There weren't any in the middle of the bay, in the swimming parts. In fact, the bay looked preternaturally clear. Obscenely blue and lovely. I laid my towel on a flat rock and rubbed sunscreen into my shoulders.

In front of me, down at the lower rocks where people dived into the water, I watched a girl in a paisley print bikini inch herself into the sea. A moment later the girl had climbed up the rocks away from the water's edge. She looked flustered, and repulsed. She had almost swum right into one.

I looked up to the cliffs and the high, battered bush. The birds were everywhere. Each year they migrated south from the sea between Japan and Alaska, down to Tasmania to breed. But there were no longer enough fish in the Bering Sea for them to eat in the northern summer. The birds became exhausted. They lost their sense of direction in the storms, and in the night they had wrecked themselves on the rocks.

I leant forward again to look at the bird. It had drifted towards the sand and the seaweed. The girl in the bikini lurched past me to where she had left her towel. We sat there, apart, each of us looking around at the massacre.

I lay on the rocks as the sun grew warmer, staring at the sea. The water was so clear in the deepest part of the bay that I could see all the way down to the sand. There was no death there. No sea snakes that I could see. When the heat got too much I stood up and picked my way down to the place where the girl had earlier stood to dive. The corpses of the birds had drifted. The bodies had washed up on the sand, where nobody lingered for long. But the scum of waste was still there. Weed and straws and Band-Aids and bottles. Sydney's great epilogue to the squall.

I slipped on the rock beneath the surface of the water and scratched myself as I slid in. I held my breath and dived beneath

the waste at the edges, swimming out into the middle of the bay. I floated.

With the water in my ears all I could hear was the thud of my heart. Bobbing there between air and water, I felt that there were no barriers between the water and me. The light pierced my eyelids. The seagulls swooped low near the rocks, feeding off the bodies of the fish, and the birds, and thrashing up the bay.

The thud of my heart. Bird cries.

There were cuts on my legs from when I'd slipped on the rocks, but the salt water didn't sting. I swam out further, away from the shore, letting the tide take me out to the threshold of the bay and the beginning of the open water. The birds called. The light dipped. No one held me back.

ACKNOWLEDGMENTS

Greatest thanks to my agent Anna Stein, and to Lucy Luck, whose encouragement, notes, and wisdom have been invaluable. Thank you to Laura Macaulay for believing in this book, and to everybody at Pushkin Press. I am ever grateful to Anne Meadows, whose notes and advice helped me give this book its final form and shape.

The Inland Sea owes much to the guidance and encouragement of my teachers in Columbia University's Writing programme, in particular Ben Metcalf, Leslie Jamison, Heidi Julavits, Rivka Galchen, and Sam Lipsyte. Thanks to Alex Abramovich for being a sounding board and a port of calm in the storm. I am especially grateful for the precious gift of space, which allowed me to finally finish this book.

I am indebted to all of those who read and offered their thoughts at various stages of the novel's composition, including Landon Mitchell, Laurel Squadron, Nicola Goldberg, Heather Radke, Tyler Parker, Lizzy Steiner, Daniel Pearce, Miles Coleman, Daniel Lefferts, Dana Hammer, and, most especially, Cam Scott. To my most cherished reader and greatest source of faith, Madelaine Lucas, I can never thank you enough.

This book is indebted to too many books and writers to list in full, but the following deserve special acknowledgment: *The Bush* by Don Watson, *The Fatal Shore* by Robert Hughes, *Sydney* by Delia Falconer, *Seven Versions of An Australian Badland* by Ross Gibson, *Journals of Two Expeditions into the Interior of New South Wales* by John Oxley, *The Water Dreamers* by Michael Cathcart, *Ecology of Fear* by Mike Davis, *The Death of Nature* by Carolyn Merchant and *The Big Ones* by Lucy Jones.

Thank you to Amina Cain, Lexi Freiman, Kristen Radtke, Josephine Rowe, Jessi Stevens, and Jeannie Vanasco.

This book is dedicated to my mother, whose support of my writing has been vital, and finally, and most importantly, to Hayden Bennett, without whom I would not have written this book.

AVAILABLE AND COMING SOON FROM

AN IMPRINT OF PUSHKIN PRESS

ONE – an imprint of Pushkin Press – is the home of our English language publishing from around the world. The list is as varied as it is distinct, encompassing new voices and established names, fiction and non-fiction. Our stories range from dystopian tales to comic ones, prizewinning novels to memoirs. And what makes them ONE? Compelling writing, unique voices, great stories.

NUMBER ONE CHINESE RESTAURANT
Lillian Li

THE OTHER'S GOLD
Elizabeth Ames

MACHINE
Susan Steinberg

SHE WOULD BE KING
Wayétu Moore

ALL YOU CAN EVER KNOW
Nicole Chung

THE INLAND SEA
Madeleine Watts

DINNER WITH EDWARD
Isabel Vincent

THE FISHERMEN
Chigozie Obioma

IN THE HOUSE IN THE DARK OF THE WOODS
Laird Hunt

ONLY KILLERS AND THIEVES
Paul Howarth

MADELEINE WATTS grew up in Sydney, Australia and has lived in New York since 2013. She has an MFA in creative writing from Columbia University, and her fiction has been published in *The White Review* and *The Lifted Brow*. Her novella *Afraid of Waking It* was awarded the 2015 Griffith Review Novella Prize. Her non-fiction has appeared in *The Believer* and the *Los Angeles Review of Books*. *The Inland Sea* is her first novel.

The item should be returned or renewed by the last date stamped below.

Dylid dychwelyd neu adnewyddu'r eitem erbyn y dyddiad olaf sydd wedi'i stampio isod.

CENTRAL.

BKEX 21·09·21

To renew visit / Adnewyddwch ar
www.newport.gov.uk/libraries